Also by Marnie Woodrow

Why We Close Our Eyes When We Kiss

In the Spice House

Marnie Woodrow

MINERVA CANADA

A Minerva Paperback
In the Spice House

First published by Minerva Canada
an imprint of Reed Books Canada.

Canadian Cataloguing in Publication Data
Woodrow, Marnie, 1969–
  In the spice house

ISBN 0 433 39839 6

I. Title

PS8595.06453I5 1996   C813'.54   C96-930111-1
PR9199.3.W66I5 1996

Printed and Bound in Canada by Webcom.

Many thanks to Oli for his faith and my editor
Suzanne Brandreth for her patience, talent and
insight. I would also like to thank my friends, without whose support and encouragement I would be
lost. They are too numerous to mention
by name... lucky me.

Eat so that you may love: love so that you may eat.

MENU

Mrs. Ann Potato

She came into the dining room wearing green velvet, cut low, and announced that she would not eat anything containing bones.

In the middle of my recital of the evening specials, she let out a horrified yelp and waved her hand frantically. I stopped, trying to determine the cause of her unrest. Her eyes bulged and she shook her cigarette at me, indicating that I had *just* said the offending something.

"Filet mignon?"

She nodded excitedly, shaking powder and perfume from her flesh.

"But ma'am—" I began to explain.

"I am completely unable to consume items that have *ever* contained bones, not just those professing to be without bones presently. I also abhor anything containing slivers of nuts, pits, seeds, or cores. Toothpicks are out of the question as well."

We agreed that her choices were excellent: the cream of mushroom soup followed by a half-portion of mashed potatoes.

"I'll have, to begin, a very *wet* martini, please. *Very* wet, and—"

"And," I interrupted sweetly, "no olive, no twist."

"Exactly!" she squealed with delight. "You're a *darling!* We're going to do very nicely together, aren't we?"

I smiled and went to the bar to order her martini. Apparently the bartender was familiar with the woman's special requirements. He scowled when I asked him to make the martini *wet*.

"I oughta put a nail in the damned thing," he muttered. "Old cow might as well have her teeth pulled out! What'd she order for dinner, oatmeal?"

When I returned to her table with the martini she was reading *A Concise History of the Eggplant* and smoking another cigarette. She beamed up at me and extended her non-smoking hand.

"I'm Ann," she said. "You'll see me here quite often. I don't know if you realize it, because you're new, but the kitchen here serves *the* finest Hollandaise sauce in the city."

"Really?" was all I could manage to say. She was completely captivating.

I found it difficult to pay attention to my other tables and stole glances at her whenever I wasn't carrying anything easy-to-spill.

And she *did* come in almost every night for dinner, from six 'til eight. She always carried a book and always wore plunged-neck dresses. She never read while eating, but instead studied every forkful before putting it into her mouth. I guessed her to be in her late fifties. There were streaks of silver in her hair and she had a speckling of liver-spots on each beautiful hand. I've always had a *thing* for liver-spots. She caught me staring at them one Wednesday evening.

"Sixty-three," she grinned. "Were you playing count-the-age-spots with me, dearest?" Her laughter rang out like a gorgeous bell and I blushed and shook my head in defense. "Honey, I'm doing well! Given the number of possible tragedies that can befall a person just *living* in this world, I am a complete success when it comes to mortality!" A darkness came into her eyes then, sudden and shadowy, and I decided that she would rather be left alone with her pudding.

"Irish coffee, Ann?" I suggested. I was still blushing guiltily but worked to recover my businesslike air. I was relieved that she had not gauged the degree to which her liver-spots stirred me.

* * *

Several evenings later my infamous and beloved Ann came into the dining room without a book. By this time I was secretly referring to her in my diary (and in my fantasies) as *Mrs. Ann Potato*. With the pseudonym I paid tribute to her favourite food and assigned her a marital status that discouraged me from expressing my attraction. I envisioned a workaholic husband whom she adored but rarely saw, a man she remained faithful to at all times, no matter how desperately lonely she became. And yet by giving her the pet-name in my head I formed an attachment to her. Never had I met a woman with such class and poise and charisma. She oozed sex and yet was completely untouchable.

Ann appeared to be a little more drunk than usual and was very conservatively dressed. I was startled by the tightly buttoned, pumpkin-coloured blouse and khaki slacks that she wore. She usually went in for much more committed shades: black and red and fuchsia; dresses with swooping necklines and slits and netting. She was showing her liver-spots and little else in the way of flesh. Her lack of reading material and sudden swing in fashion sense were causes for alarm. I greeted her warmly but received a wan smile in return.

"No menu," she sighed. "I'll have a whiskey sour, please, and hold the plastic sword."

I was deeply hurt. Here was my beloved Mrs. Ann Potato treating me like a stranger, like someone who didn't remember her special needs.

"Did something in the Hollandaise disagree with you last night, Ann?" I inquired, trying to hide my pain.

"It's a sad day, honey. An anniversary. I don't eat in restaurants on this day of the year. I can't bear to. I'm surprised I manage to eat at all anymore." She lit a cigarette and gazed at me with angst-filled eyes. "But I trust you. I trust this restaurant." Ann looked miserably at her placemat and said nothing more.

"I'm really sorry, Ann. I'll be right back with that whiskey sour, *sans* sword."

"Mmmm," she answered. Huge tears began to slide down her cheeks, cutting rivers through her pancake. I crept away, stifling my urge to hold her and console whatever sorrow was engulfing her.

"Whiskey sour, hold the sharp objects, right?" the bartender grunted. I could not understand the hostility he showed regarding Ann.

"What is it you don't like about her?" I asked, straightening my bow-tie in the mirror behind the bar.

"Listen, I've been serving that old crank drinks a long time, okay? You couldn't even *begin* to know." He shook his head; he shook the drink. He strained the drink into a glass and looked strained himself. I watched him and wondered if, after a while, all bartenders began to resemble the cocktails they made.

"What is there to dislike? She's *selective* is all," I insisted.

"*Selective?* Ha! Neurotic, maybe. Screws loose, for sure. Selective! Jesus, you got a thing for the old broad or what?" He smirked as I tore a negligent cherry from her drink.

"The word *broad* went out with the Pousse-Café," I

snapped over my shoulder, and headed toward Ann.

"What's your favourite food, angel?" she asked brightly when I set her drink down on the table.

"Excuse me?" I asked, caught off guard by the change in her mood. I didn't want to give her an answer that would upset her again. She seemed easily depressed that night and my favourite food was fried chicken. I wondered at what I might say instead and stared at her blouse for inspiration.

"The honest answer will do," she prompted.

"Pumpkin," I blurted, naming the shade of her blouse.

"Really? What an odd choice!" She smoked pensively. "And are you equally fond of squash?"

"No, I hate squash."

"Well how can *that* be? How can you adore pumpkin and hate squash?" She raised an eyebrow at me and my heart convulsed.

"How can I find one person irresistible and not be moved by another?" I dared. A man across the room was angrily waving his menu at me and I excused myself before giving in to the urge to climb onto Ann's lap.

Her mood had brightened even more when I returned to the table hoping to continue (and prolong) our conversation.

"I'm just *ravenous!*" she exclaimed, rolling the word out like an invitation. "All this booze and chit-chat have made me hungry!" She tilted her head to one side and blinked at me, "Are you a sorceress posing as a waitress?" She paused. "Because I *never* eat on this day of the year. And you've gone and lifted my spirits, and now I'm *so* hungry!"

"Would Madame care to see a menu?"

"Madame would like you to bring her whatever it is that is *really* your favourite food. Exactly how you like it prepared, with no concern for my petty fears."

"But, Ann, your dislikes are important. You shouldn't eat food you don't care for!"

"Well I *want* to. Do as I ask," she said curtly. I stood at her table trying to figure out why she was doing this to me. She looked up, surprised to see me still standing there. In a softer voice she said, "I'm sorry, angel. I didn't mean to snap. I really *do* want to try your favourite food. Whatever you like is what I'll have. Please."

On my way back toward the kitchen I thought hard about other foods I really liked. Fried chicken was just not an option. But almost everything else that came to mind had a shell, a pit, bones, seeds... It seemed to me that Ann was trying to overcome a phobia of some kind and was asking for my help. I told the chef that I needed something special for a regular customer and she nodded gladly. Any opportunity for variation on the Chenier's traditional menu was obviously welcome to her. While I waited for her to prepare the food I'd requested I went to the bar and told the bartender that *I* would be buying Ann's next whiskey sour.

"Feeling lucky?" he leered.

I leaned against the bar and fantasized that Ann would one day ask me out for drinks. I was wakened from my dream when the bartender threw a maraschino cherry at the back of my head.

"Chef's ringing you, dream-boat," he cooed.

I looked the meal over carefully before taking it out to Ann. It gave me time to summon my courage and the opportunity to drool over the choices I'd made. Everything on the plate was a carefully selected symbol of my feelings for Ann. I felt sure that she would sense the secret meaning of every item. For sentimental reasons: a dollop of whipped mashed potatoes, soft as clouds and lightly flavoured with dill. To express the tenderness I felt for her: a fan of bright green snow peas drizzled with Hollandaise. And, steaming in an intense bourbon cream sauce: a delicate and boneless breast of chicken. Though I knew she avoided meat, fish and poultry because of the bones, I felt she would see the bonelessness as a compromise. The chicken symbolized Ann's courage. The bourbon cream sauce meant business, passion, the promise of raucous pleasures to come... If she would eat the chicken she would certainly see me as her rescuer.

I set the plate before her. I looked meaningfully into the boozy sparkling eyes of Mrs. Ann Potato. She looked at the plate with initial delight: it was an aesthetic wonder and she could not deny it. Her smile quickly faded as her eyes fell upon the chicken hiding underneath its sensual sauce. A grimace of rage flew across her face and the plate hit the floor. My love-letter of a meal spattered my shoes and the fine china shattered in several directions.

There was a hoot of uncontrolled laughter from behind the bar as Mrs. Ann Potato rose from her seat and stormed out of the dining room hurling obscenities my way. Humiliation and bewilderment filled my soul as I knelt to pick the bits of china and chicken from the carpet. All eyes in the dining room were upon me. As I walked past the bar with my head held high in mock-pride, the bartender offered me his condolences.

"She's just a weird old bitch," he said. "It's happened before."

Once I had thrown away the food and the broken plate I stomped back to the bar and planted myself on one of the stools. As far as I was concerned my shift was over for the evening.

"She'll be back in tomorrow night, don't sweat it," said the bartender as he pushed a glass of red wine toward me. I lamented that she told me I could serve her whatever food I wanted to.

"I'm telling you I've seen her do it before. Same time last year, the year before that. She asks for food she never eats and then she throws it on the floor. She's got some kind of problem with food. It's not your fault. This isn't the first time, so don't take it personally."

I felt he could have spared me the humiliation and told him so. Obviously he knew what was coming.

"Hey, I never interfere with *love*. People who have the hots are *deaf*."

"I thought you just didn't like her because she's not your idea of a beautiful woman," I moaned.

"Hey, I don't care what your kink is."

"But you kept making jokes about what she likes to eat. Food is as intimate as sex for some people."

"Obviously," he teased, re-filling my glass. "Listen, I can't stand people who live in fear."

"Then I guess you can't stand most people," I hissed.

"You're right about that."

I chugged my wine and cursed myself. Wine has always made me feel sick. I wasn't really supposed to drink, but since I had already indulged, I finished off the glass anyway.

"At least Ann knows what she can't handle," I pouted, "I respect that in a person. Maybe something really terrible happened to her to make her this way..."

The bartender whipped the bar-top with his towel. "I frankly don't give two craps what *happened* to her. Get over it ! I wish everybody would just get over this past-life shit."

"Shouldn't we try to be a little more sympathetic? Maybe that's what's wrong with the world. We need to be a little more respectful of people's fears."

The bartender poured himself a double-shot of straight

vodka and banged it down. He made a terrible face and then laughed, "Well, I'm afraid of vodka. Do you respect me more now?"

* * *

A week passed and Ann did not return to the dining room of the Hotel Chenier. I gave the bartender a fresh piece of my mind, blaming him for Ann's angry exit out of my life. He reached under the bar and pulled out a newspaper, folded to a certain page. His look was sheepish and he turned his back to me as I read:

> Local socialite Ann Shadcroft was tragically killed when she was struck down by a delivery van Friday afternoon. Witnesses claim that Ms. Shadcroft left a nearby diner in a hysterical state after arguing with a waiter there. The waiter, employed by Gunny's Deli, said he could not understand Ms. Shadcroft's discontent. Shadcroft was apparently angry about the fact that she found a piece of chopped steak in her mashed potatoes. After insisting that the waiter was trying to kill her, Ms. Shadcroft became verbally abusive and would not leave the premises until the diner's owner, 88-year-old Paul Gunny, admitted that they might indeed have killed her with the piece of steak. Mr. Gunny later told the *Times* that he remembered Ms. Shadcroft's mother, a one-time regular at Gunny's. The elder Lady Shadcroft apparently choked to death in the same diner some fifty years before, a tragedy witnessed by her young daughter, Ann.

Lawyers have confirmed that Ms. Shadcroft, 63, leaves behind an estate worth over two million dollars. The sole beneficiary is a young waitress at the Hotel Chenier on Seventh Avenue whose name cannot be released until she is contacted. Family insiders describe this odd choice of bene-factor as scandalous and eccentric. A close friend of Ms. Shadcroft's commented, "I think it's great. It proves that even old Ann could find love. We had no idea that she was seeing anyone special."

Sweet Nothing

You *do* it. You *go off*, to the Arc de Triomphe and eat Chantilly cream desserts by Ferris wheels in the Paris dark. As quickly as you can, board that plane and never look back: not at the unromantic ground of Here, not at the pitiful wave that is limp from too many gestured good-byes.

Paris! I won't remind you how trite and awful the choice of Paris is as one's supposed final destination. With high drama you announce your intention to die there, but how long will it be before you are too bored to wait for Death? You'll be wearing leotards and smoking from a holder and laughing bitterly in no time. Knowing you, the best and cheapest and most gorgeous apartment in the entire City of Lights will be yours. It will face the river, look down on a bookstall, out over a bird market. I can see you already, padding around the giant flat with your cup of perfect coffee and a French newspaper you can barely read.

* * *

(on a piece of crumpled paper stolen from Bianca's waste-basket)

Dear P: Come to Paris, come to Paris, come to Paris! If you don't I'll kidnap you and marry you under my breath as we cross the Ponte de Neuf... Pack up your bag because I really don't want to go anywhere without you ever again. I will now end the torture by insisting: PARIS.

Endlessly, B.

* * *

You're reading Sylvia in a claw-foot bathtub with your edible feet pressed against the cool tiles of the wall. The water grows silky with oil and the glass of milk you add for good measure. The windows fling their arms out onto the juicy night; you read suicide poetry near an open window on the fifth floor: death has never troubled your psyche.

I challenge you to write an even more ambiguous and cruel postcard the next time you feel so inclined. Thank-you ever so much for your kind description of the Eiffel Tower. I might not have made it to my fiftieth birthday without your careful tutelage on the matter of exchange rates. Oh, and my need to understand the free-spirited habits of defecation in the pigeon species was unanswered 'til you wrote to tell. I hunger for your resolute detachment, I really do. Ache to know that you are oblivious to this old heart that sits here and simply gets older.

They say it's good luck to be shit on by a bird. May you experience a thunder-shower of good fortune on your way down every boulevard Saint whatever.

* * *

(page from Bianca's journal, discarded in the Tuilleries and found blowing in the wind)

I have fantasies that you are here. Hiding in the shrubs, or sneaking around the Marches aux Puces, wearing a disguise. Your drag is the persona of an Old French Man, a balloon vendor with a beard you stroke. You pretend to have no concern for the little girl who dances at your feet. Her awe of your magical handful of unreachable colours does not move you to lean down and tell her "They're not really for sale." You let her marvel while you stare at some imaginary vista. Her dancing becomes frantic but she is too frightened by your disinterest and can't beg out loud. Your fistful of strings, the bouquet of bouncing colours that you possess so greedily: it makes her miserable with aching. Just one balloon, Monsieur, the red one that looks like your heart... A little piece of the mesmerizing whole to carry home with her so that she can take it to her room and puncture it in a fit of beggarly sorrow.

* * *

Though you have refused me the luxury of your Parisian address and are probably busy flitting from one cabaret to another, I decide that I will find you and make you share Paris. I'm not so simple that I don't know where the airport is. And my birthday is coming. My fiftieth anniversary on this earth is the thirtieth anniversary of loving you. I'm giving myself the nicest gift I can think of: the complete dissolution of my pride.

* * *

(postcard, unmailed, in Bianca's lingerie drawer)

I've had a lot of wine and I've been listening to the Ballad of Lucy Jordan. I'm gnawing on yesterday's unfinished baguette: a dog and her bone of contention.

* * *

I could reach through the telephone wire and choke the gargoyle who pretends to be an Operator. She refuses to find your phone number and won't speak slowly. The windows in my hotel room do not swing out onto the sights and smells of Paris. They don't open at all. Despite the sullen orange of the bedspread I remain entranced by the softness of this bed. I lay on it until I can remember the name of the restaurant near your apartment. You wrote me a postcard description of your meal and mailed it without a single mention of the street where this meal was devoured. "Around the corner from where I live..." You've always preferred the general over the specific.

Bistro Liberté.

My brain is a jackpot of fragments where you are concerned. I've been granted the tragedy of a memory that hangs onto any scrap regarding you. How many meals will I have to eat at Bistro Liberté? That depends on you.

Are you still entranced by the canard fumé? Is the little table, hidden by the fountain, still a magnet for your clandestine soul? I will hide and eat. I'm sitting here where I can see you if you walk in. Your swirl of sweater and tangle of scarves, the swagger you will have forever in spite of age. The waiter notices that I have barely touched my meal and inquires, disgruntled. People come and go while I sit, putting fork-to-mouth for show.

Hurry up and get here, my birthday approaches!

* * *

(a letter mailed to P. that sits in P.'s mailbox unopened, because P. is in Paris)

P: I've decided that entertaining fantasies of our one-day togetherness is just a way in which I punish myself. While

14

such dreams are often inspiring and lead me to hopeful thoughts, it's all very unhealthy. To imagine that you will suddenly decide to love me when you probably never have is foolish.

Our history is littered with near-misses and we have taken turns guaranteeing the impossibility. I'm not dismissing your years of care, your long letters, your once-passion. But it isn't important to you anymore, and I have to accept that so I can stop longing and start living.

There will be no more wishing you were here. I refuse to dream about you, think about you, discuss you with strangers. From this day forward.

I was even foolish enough to hope you'd come here, that you could feel my desire for you over the ocean. Write me one last lovely letter and give me your good-bye. Bianca, Poste Restante.

* * *

The sky is trying not to rain and I am begging myself not to cry. The menu is filled with things I cannot eat, the streets with faces not yours. Almost everything on this menu would bring on my death upon ingestion.

"Le saumon est délicieux," says the waiter.

I'm very glad the salmon is delicious. I'm sure the wine in France is good, too, but I can't taste it. The temptation is there to just eat the things my body rejects, just so I can say I've had them again. I could subject the waiter to the scene of my demise at table, force him to dig the linen napkin from my welted fist, summon *le docteur*, too late.

I would love to taste a fine red wine on a terrasse in the Montparnasse. Just as I would love to feel you under me one last time.

In the Spice House

* * *

(note scribbled by Bianca and left with the owner of Bistro Liberté)

I know you're here. When I described you to the waiter he nodded. You remember everything, don't you? You've been eating all your meals here. Here are directions to my house. Cancel your order if you've placed one...   *B.*

* * *

The waiter, a natural born bastard, brings me a slip of paper and, holding it away from my grasp, asks, "Est-ce que vous vous appelez Phe?" He stands over me with such a smug expression that I know he has read and understood the note.

To end his surveillance of me I nod and order a glass of water with great urgency. The white of your note-paper matches the white of the tablecloth and for a second only your handwriting distinguishes it from the cloth as it lays in front of me. I am reminded of your white skin against white linen sheets... and suddenly I have two hearts for ears: one drums "Open it" and the other "Throw it away."

Tomorrow is my birthday and this note could ruin it.

I read it.

I eat it, destroying the evidence of our eternal telepathy.

I bolt from the restaurant, feeling like a revolutionary. My bayonet is the fork I still clutch in my hand. I run down the street with the directions to your house already locked in my memory. Though I've managed to lose my hotel on two occasions, even with the help of a map, I know exactly where to find you.

In the Spice House

* * *

(note pinned to the door of Bianca's flat)

Enter at own risk.

* * *

We spend a long time smoking and drinking coffee. Our mutual mourning has led us to a state of aphasia. We sit across the table from one another, delivered from temptation by a circle of wood. Sit silent, eye in eye, hand in hand. When I first arrived you kissed me in the European way, bussing each cheek. You held me at arm's length. Surveying the damage, were you?

Now you take my hands. Caress my knuckles with your absent-minded nostalgia.

"I'm sorry about my letter," you say. "I was wrong."

"Wrong about the pigeons?" I'm thinking of the postcard that enraged me.

You peer at me. "How long have you been in Paris?" You're alarmed and then glad.

"Did you write something cruel?" I reduce all things to niceness and cruelty for the sake of my nervous system. Decades of your indecision have taught me to cope this way.

You laugh and look tired, "I take it back."

Good-bye is what you have written, I can tell by the way you tighten your grip on my hands. I haven't yet received this determined farewell, this recent dismissal. Your fingers implore me to forgive you but after all these years of wanting you I am vengeful. I've always fantasized that I would be the one who was able to say it, finally. If only to be able.

"Did we really only make love once?" you ask. Your head tilts, your voice lilts, and your mouth, as always, pouts in mock-innocence and poorly-concealed lechery.

"One and a half times," I correct, and rise from the table to get away from you. The idea that you tried to say good-bye is making it difficult for me to breathe. "I think we should go out somewhere and eat. You're thin as a rake."

But it is me who weighs a pound in your presence.

* * *

(transcript of B's thoughts as they sit in a restaurant)

You come to Paris, all the way to Paris, and you want Italian food. That's the beauty of you: wherever you aren't is where you long to be. I'm sure that at this very moment you're thinking, "How nice Rome would be."

You make me laugh from the bottom of my soul with your observations of people. How have I stood the world without hearing your summaries? I've missed watching you watch. People. Me.

You decline wine. It surprises me. We've emptied many bottles of wine in our day. But you say you just don't feel like drinking. I can understand that, because I want to feel every second of our reunion, too: stone hot sober.

* * *

When the food arrives you nod at me and muster a smile, pluck cheese and bread from a plate. I used to grow weak watching you eat when we were younger. You licked everything, drove your teeth deep into every bite. When you got married and we decided we shouldn't *make love ever again* (our words), I contented myself with watching you eat. By the end of every meal with you I was sick with desire but so strangely satisfied, too, just to have eaten in your company.

With careful fingers you extract the naked pit of an olive from your mouth. Its black and salty flesh is gliding down your throat. You hand me an olive, or rather, you place one against my lips and giggle when I take it into my mouth along with one of your fingers. The people at the table next to ours are staring, and who wouldn't, because when we dine together we are rather beautiful in our gluttony.

Are there tears in your eyes? You're upset so suddenly after laughing so gleefully. I roll the olive in my mouth, unconsciously stripping away its flesh as I watch your eyes brim. I want to say something, and so I pluck the pit from my mouth and set it on the plate, and try to take your hand.

"I wish I was an olive," you say with sudden volume. How is it that you do that? With simple strings of words you deftly halt the machinations of my lungs. Our main dishes arrive and we eat them without care, pay for them, depart.

We're in *Paris*, I think as we walk briskly back to your apartment. We climb the eight thousand stairs and this is Paris, but it might be anywhere. The city itself is not responsible for the electric swoon in the air between us. It would be like this in Ohio. *Has been* like this in Ohio. In shopping malls, diners, in the zoo of places we have strolled through together.

But I tell myself it's because it's Paris that I can't wait to get you upstairs and hold you hostage in my arms. In this city of revolutions, of resistance, it seems only proper to storm the invisible barricades between you and me.

In the Spice House

* * *

(on a slip of paper tucked in the corner of Bianca's bureau mirror)

> *(i do not know what it is about you that closes*
> *and opens;only something in me understands*
> *the voice of your eyes is deeper than all roses)*
> *nobody,not even the rain,has such small hands*

—e.e. cummings

* * *

I've made a number of promises to myself and broken them all. When I boarded the plane to come here I told myself I would never kiss you again. But here we are on your sofa and one glance at your lips destroys my reserve. When I sat in my hotel on the first night I vowed that I would never feel your stomach against mine, *ever again.* But here we are, all tongue-and-hipbone, belly to belly.

Now I'm sprawled here with your hair spread across my chest and I'm making a promise to myself that can't be broken. I'm counting on your faulty memory and your ego in the kitchen. I make a shopping list in my head as I run my fingers over your innocent eyelids. There is no more room in my heart for disappointment.

* * *

(Bianca's monologue, written on the inside of her head)

I remember the way you could send me a piece of you in the
mail and how even my delight at the sight of your hand-writ-

ing was smashed by your insistent resistance. Letters, never cards, always with your full-out wishing and postulating, the tiny cursive crowbars that pried into my heart... You kept telling me of your regret but never offered a remedy.

We sent that poem back and forth to one another for years; no matter where I went I took it with me, in chunks or in its perfect wholesome form. You kept writing it out, underlining the particularly damning or blessed lines that best described our bisected togetherness. Reminding me of what I couldn't have, and of what I couldn't give.

And now I've got you here in my apartment and I can't keep you here, won't even try. You'll never let go of your mythology that I am the one who will break your heart. Not even romantic Paris will weaken you. The thought of losing you again is unbearable. I can't even bear to entertain the scene and so I think about our next meal, the music I'll play, the things I could say to seduce you so finally that you wouldn't need to leave me .

* * *

Here is the list: salmon, red wine, green grapes, cold smoked oysters, blueberry cheesecake.

You come back from shopping and lay them out on the counter and begin to work your magic. I'm over here in the jungle of books and records you've collected and set on shelves with the carelessness that has always made you perfect. Your reckless decoration of any home reveals your unwillingness to settle. And there's one more thing I love: even when plants die you keep them in their pots. They curl and petrify in their clay graves and you cherish them as though they are still alive. No wonder you can still love me.

* * *

(what Bianca paused to write on the back of P.'s shopping list while out in the market)

I think we should eat on the terrace so I can jump to my death after dinner. I want to be the first to go. You'll weather my departure better than I would suffer yours.

As for the music I'll play: Goldberg Variations. How well I remember that one afternoon of rain and arching backs. We drank cold coffee and mashed our cigarettes out on a pie-plate. The bed was a magnet and Mister Gould hummed in the background. The cassette never ended.

You say we made love one and a half times, but I can't recall any half-way anything about us... Even our cowardice has been full-out passionate...

* * *

The table is set, the music is on and it finally feels like my birthday. The apartment is filled with smells: of broiling salmon, of cologne atomized in another room, of flowers, dust, candles sweating out tears of wax. Paris clatters in the street below. It's a city like all others, noisy with horns and business. Sitting expectantly at your table I am aware of the sweetness of our togetherness but not of the locale. I certainly never dreamed of celebrating my birthday in Paris but here we are. Watching you balance the tray of food, I know we should have been like this everywhere.

* * *

(written on the inside of a birthday card for P. that rests against the pillows of Bianca's bed)

P: Here we are. Your birthday is at long last MINE. I'd like to make a reservation for the next one hundred birthdays.

* * *

"You're eating so fast," I remark, watching you wolf. Whereas you have always sucked and savoured, you now make a New York lunch of our fabulous feast.

"Sorry," you giggle, tucking an escapee bit of oyster back into your mouth, "I'm nervous."

Nervous? I can't believe that you, always placid and together you, are nervous. I'm reveling in my every languid chew and holding foods in my mouth that I'd forgotten the taste of. I feel calm and joyful and request more wine.

You mustn't notice my determined wish to make sure. That I have second helpings of everything, even dessert. Your gluttony focusses itself on the wine. I lose count of the glasses that slide down my own throat and yet I notice that you are drinking faster and with more distraction than you used to.

"Your face is all flushed," you murmur, and take my hand. Our bones jigsaw with such perfection. The insistence of your thumb on mine brings back every ancient desire. "Can I ask you something?"

Because I have the beginnings of a coil of wool in my throat, a constriction I don't want you to hear, I just nod. My blood flows in a hot confusion of desire and panic. Deep inside my lungs and capillaries, my body's rejection of the meal is beginning.

"Can we go to bed? *Now?*" You've never been so direct. Questions and answers never before so important to you.

In the Spice House

(printout from Bianca's central nervous system)

I know it's obvious: the lamp glowing on the night-table, the sheets turned down. So blatant in my desire to get you back into bed. There are so many things I want to tell you. I should just give you the birthday card and let you figure it out. That this is the last time I can offer you Forever. But you don't want to read cards. You push the card away and pull me to the bed.

* * *

Though I've dreamt for years of making love to you again and talking to you the whole time, I find I have to be silent. To speak is to acknowledge the difficulty I'm having breathing. I don't want you to know that anything is wrong. You think my red flesh is the result of desire, that my swollen mouth is a side-effect of years of pent-up lust. Even through the itching of my skin I am mesmerized by the silk of you, your every touch. Where you dig your hands into my back, welts appear. The thunder of your breathing masks my own laboured inhalations. In your passion you don't hear the papery rasp of my lungs.

* * *

(in Bianca's head)

I'd forgotten the drastic heat of you, your make-believe patience, the exactitude of your every dream-like push. You breathe so beautifully, like every inward pull of air is your last...

In the Spice House

In your shuddering you don't feel my own: the dimming spin of the lights, the drifting away of your skin, the last vestiges of your perfume slipping into the cobweb network of my lungs. You lock your hands around the back of my neck, press my sweltering cheek to your hips. You hold me like this and have no idea of the happy ending you provide.

"Sweet everything," you whisper. We used to finish phonecalls with those words, never saying *good-bye* out of superstition.

I'm not there to feel your panicked slaps of attempted revival or hear you swearing through streams of angry tears. Not there to sit with you in the hours of silence that follow your discovery. Thoughtful you, you don't call an ambulance, you simply clear the table and throw our plates out of your Paris window. I'm not there to grieve the furied choice you make.

* * *

(on a piece of paper found crumpled and soaked with wine on the floor of Bianca's bedroom, in front of the open window)

Sweet nothing... it's been a too-long life without you.

32 Flavours

"What flavours do you have?" This question posed as the man in the ugly cardigan stands below the sign that lists all thirty-two flavours of ice-cream. A scream wells inside the clerk but she stifles it and begins:

"Black Cherry, Choklit Bomber, Lemon Sherbet, Icy Mint Fudge, Smoking Gun, Dripping Dagger, Smashed Skull, Pureed Cranium..."

The man in the cardigan turns pale. He is a Customer. He is frightened by the girl behind the counter of 32 Flavours. She *seems* normal: pony-tail, red lips, nice tits. But she is odd, and what she says is definitely bizarre and almost... *violent.*

"Excuse me?" the man asks, completely indignant. He can't believe this girl would really be so rude to a Customer.

"Chocolate Asshole, Severed Head Surprise, Death Valley Swirl, Bye-Bye Bastard Custard—"

"You're *sick!*" snaps the man. He quickly puts his money back into his wallet and storms out of the air-conditioned cool of the 32 Flavours. On the sidewalk, collecting his wits, he vows to call the Manager on Monday morning to complain. He might very well contact the 32 Flavours Head Office and demand an apology and gift certificate. By fax and by phone he will make sure that the girl is fired. All he had wanted was a little ice-cream cone and he had received this... *anger* instead. This unwarranted, perverse anger.

27

The girl wiped the sticky counter with a warm wet cloth. She smiled to herself and changed the water in the bucket where the scoops were kept. Kept wet to make the scooping easier. She knew what a joke that concept was. Even if the scoops were heated to 400°F, the ice-cream still wouldn't budge from the rock-hard paper tubs. It was either dripping all over everything or it had to be blasted out with a hammer and chisel. She hated scooping ice-cream for a living. It aggravated her and made her think violent thoughts. She was convinced that most serial killers had at one time in their lives been food service workers. It would explain a lot. The sticky gumminess that coated her arms from her finger-tips to her armpits got on her nerves. Once she had actually found a piece of cookie from Kooky Kookie lodged in her underarm. It disgusted her, all of it, but it was her job. She was poorly paid but, like thousands of other retail employees, her self-esteem had been shot to shit by the management practices of 32 Flavours and she was afraid to quit. There weren't too many jobs out there: she was lucky to even *have* a job. Chanting about Hard Times was the Manager's favourite way to crush her dream of ever quitting.

She decides one afternoon that the next idiot who orders Bubblegum ice-cream and wears his baseball cap backwards will really get it. The full blast of her building rage. There is a big red callous on her thumb from digging into flavours like that, the ones filled with obstructions: Candy Cane, Crunchy Crunch, Bubblegum. On busy afternoons the callous bleeds, soaking the rag she wraps around the scoop handle to increase traction. Picking sugar from the split-ends of her pony-tail, she fantasizes that it is December. Summer is hell at 32 Flavours. In December she can read books and daydream, and hardly anyone but the odd freak bothers her. In winter the shifts are shorter and her hands don't hurt as much. She doesn't feel quite as angry in the winter.

The gelati flavours are kept in an upright display freezer behind her. Sometimes, whirling around to yank the doors open, she sees herself refelcted in the glass. A quick, blurry, horror-movie of a girl with a blunt silver object in one hand and a sugar cone in the other. There she is: a true-crime reading, ice-cream scooping, angry young woman.

She has a boyfriend, of sorts. He skis all winter and sails all summer. He is an absentee boyfriend. It works for her, and fulfills her mother's expectations. She has a friend, Wendy Carmichael, who comes by the store to visit with a Thermos-full of Margaritas. Wendy feels sorry for the girl, and brings the drinks to soothe her frazzled nerves. After a few belts of Margarita, Wendy takes the girl into the back freezer and kisses her. They kiss until the next hoard of ice-cream licking pigs marches in. The girl doesn't have time to question why she loathes her boyfriend and keeps kissing Wendy back. It's July. The bastards want their ice-cream.

She hits the jack-pot one day: a creepy engineering student comes in with his frat-hat on backwards. It's cherry-coloured courduroy. He is leering, strutting, doing her a favour by smiling at her. Pretending to be boyish and innocent, a young lad in search of a nice ice-cream cone to molest with his beer-soaked tongue.

He shuffles his feet, pretends he is bashful. He orders Bubblegum ice-cream. She snaps.

* * *

Wendy comes in that night with her Thermos. The 32 Flavours is quiet, an odd thing for a Saturday night in July.

The girl is nowhere to be seen behind the counter. The fridges hum, the air-conditioning is on too high. It's all normal, all the same except for a lack of Customers. Wendy looks down the hall that leads to the walk-in freezer at the back of the store. Seeing no sign of her friend, she sits down at one of the little purple tables and waits.

When the girl finally emerges from the back room she is smiling. She wears a look of satisfaction Wendy has never seen before. It makes Wendy uneasy.

"Hi Wen!" The girl is positively singing. She begins wiping down all of the counters, whistling a tune. When she looks up at Wendy, Wendy is staring down the hall that leads to the walk-in.

"Is there someone else here?" Wendy asks, trying to sound casual. After all, the girl has every right to entertain whomever she pleases in the walk-in freezer of the 32 Flavours.

"Of course not," says the girl brightly.

"Well... you seem kind of... uhm... happy. It's weird."

The girl nods and smiles. "I've discovered the secret to enjoying my job. I read a book last night, *Do What You Love, Love What You Do, Too*. It talks a lot about anger and how it can ruin your job and your life if you let it. If you don't find a way to *channel* it. I've channelled! I'm thinking I might even buy a 32 Flavours franchise someday."

"What?" Wendy gasps.

"I am in control of my work experience. I have one life. I have to make the most of it. There are benefits to this job that I wasn't able to recognize before. I have taken control of my work experience tonight. Let me show you..." She takes Wendy's hand and leads her toward the walk-in freezer.

"Hang on a sec!" Not even Wendy's amorous excitement can make her leave her Thermos behind on the table.

It is the first time that the girl is taking the initiative and is leading the way to the freezer. She doesn't seem drunk or high. It is a sober decision and one that makes Wendy's heart swoon. Before she opens the freezer door the girl gives Wendy a long and wonderful look. There is a new spark in the girl's eyes. Wendy leans forward and kisses her impulsively. The girl loosens her pony-tail and shakes her hair free.

"I hate scooping ice-cream, Wendy. I can't tell you the kind of rage that builds inside me after an hour or two of scraping at those buckets. The sickly-sweet smell, the air-conditioning. I've had a cold for three and a half years! It eats away at a person. Tonight I embraced the rage."

"You finally told a Customer to fuck off, didn't you?" Wendy squeals. "Way to go! They're all so rude to you, the pigs! Making you recite the flavours, all thirty-two!"

"That isn't what happened," the girl begins, but the bells on the front door clatter and she has to go out front. Wendy waits in the hallway with her Thermos, listening.

A family of three stands impatiently in the store, craning their necks as though they have been waiting there for several weeks instead of the few seconds that have passed. The girl appears, smiling. She offers each member of the family a free sample. The three of them smack their lips and make some of the most offensive noises the girl has ever heard. The ratty-wigged wife orders Low Fat Berry and then waves it away when the girl tries to hand it to her over the counter.

"Too runny," she whines, "gimme Choklit Bunny!"

The husband snorts, "From Low Fat to So Fat!"

He stands and scratches his red beard, gazing up at the flavour list with matching red eyes. He ponders and sighs. The girl feels her old agitation building. She looks down at the little boy and he begins to bellow his order out but is silenced by a slap from his father.

"Daddy first!" the well-trained wife screeches between slurps of her cone.

"Hmmmm. Uh. Let me see now. Thirty-two flavours, eh? It's hard to know."

"Lemon?" the wife suggests.

"SHUT UP!" he roars.

There is silence now, nothing but the whir of the freezers, the fan, the metallic wheezings of the air conditioner.

"Sir?" the girl prompts.

"Just a goddamn minute!" the man snaps. He glares over the napkin dispenser at her.

"Daaaaaddd!" the little boy whines.

"Gaarrry, please!" the wife chimes.

The husband puffs up his chest and purses his lips into a thin, mean line. Slowly he raises one hair-coated arm and points to the door. "Do you want to go to the CAR?" he threatens his family.

The wife and little boy shake their heads and shrink down, waiting. The man turns back to the list of flavours. The girl hears the sound of the walk-in freezer door opening and her heart begins to pound. Wendy.

"Which one do *you* like?" the man asks, staring at the girl's breasts through the display-case windows.

The girl's face goes hot with rage and she says quietly, "I'm vegan."

"WHAT?" the man shouts, leaning far over the counter, as far as he can manage.

"I'm waitin'," the girl answers, stepping back from his sweating face.

"I'll have..." he licks his beefy lips, "I think I'll have... vanilla. VANILLA. S'at okay with you?"

The girl calls out to Wendy. She is hanging by her last

nerve-ending. Wendy comes out from the back freezer with an ice-cream scoop in her hand.

"What'd he order?" she demands.

"After several moments of deliberation: vanilla," the girl whispers.

She snaps. Wendy snaps with her. The scoops fly and dagger.

* * *

Wendy and the girl sit in the walk-in freezer with the Thermos of Margaritas. They watch the little boy gleefully eating an entire tub of Banana Cloud. His legs are tied up but his arms are free.

"What was it that got you the first time?" Wendy asks.

"Bubblegum."

"I can see how that would do it. Plus that hat. The hat is a definite agitator."

The two girls look over at the place on the freezer floor where they have piled the bodies of the frat boy, the wife and red-bearded husband. The bodies are stiffening in the cold of the freezer. They have spared the little boy, being optimistic at the bottom of their souls. It isn't the little boy's fault that his parents are Bad Customers.

"Are you going to quit?" Wendy asks.

The girl swigs Margarita and lets it splash down the front of her. Other splashes on her t-shirt have begun to freeze. She feels reckless and wild. *Free.*

"Well, my boss is on vacation. And we just had inspection. I'm running the place for another couple of weeks at least. I think I should stick around."

"I think you should hire me!" Wendy exclaims.

"Well, I will need help," the girl nods, "there are still twenty-nine flavours to go!"

At this the girls howl, clinking their bloodied scoops together.

"How's your Banana Cloud?" Wendy asks the little boy.

"Very good, thank-you!" he answers, his mouth full.

"You're on the right road," the girl smiles, "Always be a Good Customer, okay?"

King Cake

Whoever finds the baby in their King Cake has to throw the next party.

She and his wife are shooting tequila, banging down the glasses and making faces. They lean on the bar-top and on one another while he smokes and watches from a shadow-black corner.

Mardi Gras is coming and they want to show her how to celebrate it right. With cocktails and music and all the right rituals. Bombs of beads are bursting in the air; a never-ending parade marches through her head. She has been in New Orleans for a few months, seen Thanksgiving and Christmas blur by in a fury of deep-fried turkeys and booze and commonplace hedonism. But Mardi Gras will be the insane climax to a year-round build-up of everyday celebration. The *joie de vivre* needs to explode. After Mardi Gras she will extract herself and go back home. As a farewell gesture, her boss and his wife will guide her through her very first Mardi Gras.

The ritual: eating cake dyed purple and gold, royal colours for a King Cake. Inside the cake, baked some-where inside, a tiny glass baby is waiting to be found. One bites carefully, hunting with the teeth in tentative nibbles. Some party hosts prefer to use a plastic baby that is pushed into the cake after baking. But the cake they are eating on this particular night at this particular bar-party is mother to a fragile glass baby. The traditional way. The cake is

35

served and everyone indulges, taking drunken care not to chomp down and shatter the prize.

His wife encourages her to have another drink. Someone further down the bar is buying a round for the house. She is already seeing two shimmering versions of everything but it seems ridiculous to decline an offer of further excess in a bar called Bacchus. Over in the corner her boss rolls joints without watching his hands. He watches his wife and the young woman who works for him and feels the snake in his belly coil tight 'til it rattles. His wife is listening to the young woman, who leans in close and brushes her lips against the curls of his wife's hair. They are drunk and this is a party, but there is something ugly about the way the Yankee girl whispers to his wife.

When the joints are rolled he moves toward the bar, slowly so as not to disturb their conversation. His wife can't be trusted when left alone, and it is by sneaking up on her in crowds that he learns what she is up to. On more than one occasion he has learned that she is a liar, a cheat, and sometimes, when she is very drunk, that she hates him.

Countless times he has been forced to take her home and set her straight: *Women are like children, darlin'. They need discipline.*

The two women are speaking so quietly that he can't catch a word from a safe distance. They are being especially careful, not letting a single word float away. He watches as they lean into each other, conspiring. The snake inside him grows tighter and meaner. He grabs two more pieces of King Cake from the buffet table and marches toward them wearing a festive grin.

"Well, hello ladies! Think you'd like some solid food to help wash down that liquor?"

His wife spins around sharply on her bar-stool, a dangerous maneouvre given the number of drinks she has consumed. "You're only s'posed to have one piece each," she reminds him.

"I won't tell a soul," he whispers, and winks at the young woman, ignoring his wife.

Whenever he winks at her she feels sick to her stomach. The first few times she let it go, thinking it was some kind of southern male tradition, an innocent display of meaningless affection. When it continued and was accompanied by lewd grins, it began to fill her with dread. As he pushes the second piece of cake at her she is glad to be leaving New Orleans right after Fat Tuesday.

Without any kind of warning his wife excuses herself and swerves toward the Ladies' Room, leaving her alone with her sober boss and his unsettling stare. She accepts the second piece of cake to placate him. One was always placating him it seemed. She bites down carefully.

"Sure would love it if you had to throw the next party, darlin'," he whispers.

If you *had* to...

"Now just what were you two girls talkin' about over here so serious and quiet? This is a party! Down here we like to enjoy ourselves. You ladies oughta' learn to loosen up a little. Shit, no woman seems to know how to have fun anymore!" He works the toothpick between his teeth too furiously. She wonders if it is the booze or the sugary cake that is making her heart pound so jaggedly. His wife seems to be taking forever in the washroom.

"Find that baby yet?" he asks suddenly, just as her teeth touch down on something harder than cake. Her tongue discovers the dull smoothness of the waxed paper that the baby is wrapped in. She shakes her head NO and pretends to chew, takes a huge swig of her drink. She swallows the paper-wrapped baby in one giant ragged gulp, and bites into the cake again for show. In an effort to look like she is still hoping to find the baby, she wears a cautious expression as she chews.

When his wife returns he whirls around and asks *her* what the two of them had been discussing. She smiles weakly and tugs at a package of cigarettes in his breast-pocket, but he swats her hand away.

"About her leaving," his wife insists, "I told her she should stay."

"I think she should stay, too, baby, but you can't force these young gals to do anythin', can you?" He looks hard at the young woman and his eyes glitter serpentine. She has always struck him as being willfull. Too. "Let's get you home," he announces suddenly, his eyes dead and expressionless as he tugs on his wife's arm. He continues to stare at the young woman. Though he looks at her, he doesn't *see* her. He sees a version of her that suits him.

The three of them squeeze through the sweating crowd, crushed by the slick of bodies and smoke. The man waves to several people, but he never takes his other hand off his wife's arm. The room is so hot, and so stifling, that when they burst out into the cool courtyard full of blossoms, it seems as though a sudden gift of air has been given.

"Oxygen!" the young woman exclaims, taking this opportunity to walk ahead of the couple.

She makes a grand show of breathing in the cool night air and the perfume of the flowers. It is incongruous that such a grimy and smoke-filled bar could have such a paradisical courtyard. The music from inside the bar can be heard, a faint and festive thumping checkered with lunatic hoots. He sits down on a wooden bench beneath a vine-covered arbour and slaps his knees gleefully. He grins at the two women as they stagger about the yard and look pleadingly at him.

"C'mon, let's go," his wife begs. "This cold air's makin' me drunk."

The man shakes his head and laughs, "You girls got to learn to slow down on the booze! Shoulda' paced yourselves. I just want to smoke a little joint before we drive our friend here all the way back down to the Marigny. You two've had *your* fun. I've been behavin' myself all night." He lights the joint and pats the bench, indicating that the women should sit down and wait. His wife swears under her breath but goes to the bench obediently. In the pit of her belly the young woman is sure she can feel the glass baby lolling around, unwrapping itself. She takes a seat next to her boss and tries not to breathe in. The smell of him bites through the blossoms above her head.

"Toke?" he asks, holding out the joint, and she obliges, sitting in the garden of the Bacchus bar.

Whoever finds the baby in their piece of King Cake has to throw the next party.

Whoever finds it and swallows it and lies about finding it, thus denying everyone else at the party their fun, must pay a price. Bacchus charges a high price for the denial of pleasure.

The snake in his belly knows all about the baby and where it is and who is lying about it. He saw her gulping her drink. He will collect the fee for Bacchus.

The snake in his belly knows that people beg his wife to leave him, urge her and tempt her with offers of refuge.

The snake knows who will throw the next party. No one can stop the God of Pleasure from getting what he wants.

The young woman wakes up the way one wakes up after a night of heavy drinking and smoking and cake-eating. She blinks her swollen eyes and is unaware of the rest of her body. She is a head on a pillow: a pounding, bodiless skull.

She takes a deep breath and smells two things: dog-piss and man-sweat.

She doesn't have a dog.

She doesn't sleep with men.

She sits up so fast that her skullbones begin to burn. She is completely naked, covered by a thin blanket, on someone else's couch. She isn't at home, though she was promised that she would get there.

She looks around and shakes her head to make the hallucination stop. Grabs for her clothes, a memory, for a sign that she is dreaming. But there is a smell on her hands. The stink of nervous sweat and sharp, masculine cologne.

In a bathroom down a hallway, she tries to piss. There is blood, a searing pain deep in her, and yet, no memory. Her face hurts. Her mind screams but her throat is bone-dry. She stumbles back to the living room, every step agonizing and filled with the smell. The house is silent: is anyone home? She has no voice to call out with. Realization comes in glimmers: her face hurts across the bridge of her nose, she recalls a hand holding her head down, pushing hard on her face. Blackness. A saw-blade going in and out of her. She listens, terrified to be alone, alarmed by the thought of company. She vomits on the coffee table in front of her and begins to sift through the muck with her hands, searching frantically for the little glass baby. There is only liquid, sour and hot. She sifts and sifts, desperate for even the smallest piece of waxed paper to prove she isn't dreaming. There is nothing.

When his wife appears in the doorway of the living room, the young woman isn't surprised to see her. His wife sees the table covered in vomit and begins to swear. She shakes her head. The young woman tries to tell her what he has done but her voice refuses to come out. When his wife turns to go back down the hall the young woman waves her hands.

"Leave him," she croaks. More vomit comes and she doesn't bother to put her hands up to her face. It won't do any good to put her hands up.

"We went through all this last night," his wife groans.

When the young woman begins to weep uncontrollably his wife clucks her tongue in disgust.

"You took your own clothes off," she says suddenly, and disappears down the hall.

Somewhere, in another unseen room, there is the sound of someone opening and closing closets. The smell of coffee floats toward the young woman on the couch. The wife feels badly about speaking so roughly to her. She brings her a pair of sunglasses and a cup of coffee. They sit sipping coffee beside the table covered in vomit, pretending not to notice it.

The wife calls a taxi and the two women leave the house wearing matching sunglasses. It makes an odd picture. The wife is on her way to work in the French Market. She sells sunglasses and cheap wallets to tourists. The taxi drops the young woman off on the corner near her apartment building. His wife waves but she doesn't notice because her sunglasses are too dark.

There is a message waiting on her answering machine when she enters the apartment.

"You threw a real nice party, darlin'."

He calls again but she doesn't answer the phone. She hears his voice on the machine, "Drop by the bar before you leave town. I'll buy you some cocktails. I know how you like those cocktails."

Over the course of the afternoon he leaves eight more messages; gloats into her machine, his voice becoming more and more uncertainly pleased with every taunt.

She packs her bags and moves around the apartment, collecting mementoes. She decides to leave the city that night to avoid running into him in the streets. Mardi Gras isn't that important to her, she thinks. Terrible cramps overcome her and she runs to the bathroom. Her bowels explode.

* * *

When she finds the perfect jar she fills it with as much shit as she can salvage. It doesn't make her queasy at all. She drops the little glass baby into the jar. It has passed safely through her without breaking: one miracle. She makes sure it is visible through the glass of the jar and attatches a note to the lid.

On her way to the Greyhound station she tells the cab driver to wait while she runs into the bar. She carries the jar, wrapped in a brown paper bag and addressed to him, into the crowded front room. The bar will be busy when he picks up his package and she counts on him to open it right away.

She has written, in big red letters, on a piece of paper glued to the lid:

R A P I S T

She can't help his wife. She probably should have gone to the police but she has met the police before. The jar-gesture will have to suffice. For now. He'll do it again, to someone else, but she can't prevent that. She can only try to stop the way she feels.

She calls her own phone-number from a payphone at the bus station. The machine kicks in and she knows it is full of the sound of him. She adds one more message:

"The man whose voice is on this machine owns the Heartache Bar. He is a rapist."

On the bus she prays that the taste of that cake will one day leave her mouth. And she weeps every minute of the twenty-seven Greyhound hours home, angry that she has to pray at all.

Suck

I lived a good life in my cheffy whites without too much trouble. I was good-cooking in some pretty swanky kitchens, here and there, north-south; fresh out of college and ready to take on the food-world. It's true, I was always some man's sous-slave or low-rung assistant, waiting in the wings. And it grinds on the nerves, slavery does, and can lead to unusual thoughts. Yet everyone I have known in the world of food says that it is all worth it in the end, when you have paid your dues and freedom comes.

In New Orleans I found freedom. I was appointed head chef of a nouveau-respectable restaurant. I topped my head with the tallest of white hats. There I was, steering my own spoon, pointing my own cleaver, criticizing my own errors for a change. The restaurant catered to the transient celebrities that float in and out of that city: the easily wooed, the over-socialized adult children of rich parents, gangster-janitors, ex-Hollywooders. I would make the special dishes they requested, oversee the nourishment of the jet-set brats who thought it quaint to try gumbo. I would work the long hours and go to market myself, budget and menu-make and in between, whip up a celebrity-pleasing étouffée or two.

As a woman, it was expected that I would keep my skilled self tucked away in the confines of the kitchen. I was asked to avoid the dining-room showboating of certain local male chefs. If, for some reason a patron really wanted to speak to me at her table, I was to change my apron, apply lipstick and keep my thank-yous and how-tos short and southern-belle sweet. That I was a northerner and about as un-belle as they come made no difference to the owner, whose firm belief it was that people disapproved of Lady Chefs.

Instead of going to the trouble of applying lipstick and fluffing my hair, I pretended to be seriously shy, a borderline agoraphobic, one cozier in her kitchenette. It really didn't matter to me one *soupçon* what the patrons thought about Lady Chefs, but I complied by making myself seem clinically unavailable to the public. I played the role of a mystery-chef with a medical inability to *chat*.

Months after I began to cook at the said Bistro de, I was informed that a certain film actress had made a reservation. A famous workaholic, she was a personal heartthrob of mine. I was thrilled to have the opportunity to cook for, and hopefully meet, her. This was one time when I planned to make my presence felt table-side. There would be no skulking around the kitchen for me during her visit. She apparently wanted to try crawfish, as she was preparing for a role in a movie set in Mississippi. The heroine would naturally subsist on a diet of crawfish for breakfast, lunch and dinner, and so the actress wanted to master the fine art of craw-eating before filming began.

I was pleased to oblige her artistic dedication and drove to Biloxi myself on the afternoon of her reservation to procure the finest crawfish available. They were sold in large plastic bags on the side of the highway and were best served after a quick-boil and liberal seasoning. As I flew back along the Gulf Coast highway I felt sure that this simple meal would be one of my most important culinary experiences, and that my life was about to change in profound ways.

On that day I refused to allow any other members of the staff to assist me. I wanted complete control over every detail and locked my assistants out of the kitchen for most of the afternoon. There would be a wonderfully mucky Dijon potato salad, a creation I had received many compliments on in the past. While the salad sat and creamed-'n-onioned itself to perfection, I shucked corncobs for the starlette and her three unknown friends. There was a strange knotting in my gut as I shucked, a titillation that shivered through me with the stripping away of each green leaf. I blamed my excitation on my star-struck ways, for I could think of no other time when the preparation of a meal had moved me so.

Maybe on a few other nights, in a few other lesser-known restaurants, there had been occasional feelings of stimulation. Nothing quite as profound as the raw excitement I felt on crawfish night, but I have always enjoyed watching people eat the food I cook. It seems perfectly natural to me that a chef would derive great pleasure from watching diners smack their lips in gourmandly delight. Doesn't it make the endless hours labouring in hot kitchens and the lack of social life worth it, after all? Even in my early days as a short-order cook in a greasy spoon, I found that a glimpse of happy people eating one of my finely-crafted grilled cheese sandwiches put a song in my spatula. I always thought the tingle in my trousers was confirmation of my destiny as a chef.

A pot of spicy water boiled next to me, shuddering in its own anticipation. Cayenne steam-clouds caressed my cheeks as I leaned over the pot, inhaling the perfumes of pepper and onion. I took the sack of crawfish out of the fridge and dumped them into a large colander. It would be pure heaven to finally plunge their perfectly curling craw-bodies into the rolling water. I fingered their lovely red shells, marveling at the perfection of size and colour. I felt sure that the actress would devour them with fascination and horror. And *I* would be the one to teach her just how to eat crawfish; how to squeeze the head and suck the juice. She would probably thank me along with the Academy for helping to make her performance in the film more authentic. My head swam with fantasies.

Because I am discreet, even now when I have no cause to be, I will not tell you the name of that actress. She has always been an extremely private person. I'm sure that she still is. Perhaps she doesn't even dine in restaurants any-more...

The rest of my staff were allowed back into the kitchen and there was a buzz of quiet excitement. The owner informed me that her car had arrived and that their coats were at last checked. The party of four were soon deep into their cocktails and before-dinnerisms. We teased them with a basket of hushpuppies and deep-fried oysters. My hands shook as I plunged the succulent shellfish into the boil. The waiter announced that the main course could be served and he slumped impatiently. When I informed him that *I* would be delivering the crawfish plat-ter myself, and that he could follow with the corn and potato salad, he shot me a hateful look. I couldn't help but smile.

"Please," I said, taking up the platter, "I've seen GIRL COP *eleven* times. I have no intention of missing this."

There was no time for further disagreement. I marched into the dining room with the platter held high. I was without lipstick, unfluffed. My apron was stained and my hat was askew and my heart pounded like a thing untamed beneath my jersey as I spotted the table and *she*.

Quietly and wordlessly I moved to one side of her chair. I took up a crawfish from the pile. She looked up at

me with a curious smile and nodded as I began to demon-
strate how one peels away the sections of the back. How
then to yank the head with the free hand, tugging the
meat while pinching the tail. I did it swiftly and deftly
despite the trembling of my fingers. After devouring the
meat I held the head of the crawfish in my hand, careful
not to spill the juices.

"And what do you do with *that?*" she demanded, grinning and pointing at the head. Admittedly, some people
find the sight of the dislodged head a bit garish and unap-
petizing, but I could see that she was a woman whose
curiosity made her barbaric.

I looked around at the faces of her companions: all of
them eager and silk-shirted, one appalled but hiding his
disgust behind a martini. I tipped my head back and put
the craw-skull to my lips, sucking loudly. As I pinched the
head the juices of the brain gushed into my mouth and,
with all of the gentility I could muster, I placed the skele-
ton and skull neatly on the sheet of newspaper provided
and curtsied, leaving the actress and her friends stunned
and giddy.

As I retreated to the kitchen I heard my beloved starlet
exclaim loudly, "What a town!" and then, "More drinks!"

There was a thundering in my ears as I made my way
back through the kitchen. The sous-chef watched me carefully. For a few minutes I made a grand show of delivering
dirty dishes to the dish-boy, but I could stand it no longer.
I think my face must have been crawdaddy red as I went
to the kitchen door and stared through the round window
that looked out into the dining room. Their table was just
visible. The actress took up a crawfish and was ambitious-
ly peeling and digging her thumbs into the shell of the
fish. She laughed wildly, a laugh that flew through the
linen-velvet hush of the dining room. Juice ran down the

front of her blouse but she hardly seemed to care. Eventually, after a great struggle, the meat slid cleanly out of the shell and she cheered, victoriously popped the morsel into her mouth and grabbed for another.

Behind me the clatter-bashing of pots seemed miles away. I watched her spirited feasting with a keen sense of desire. It thrilled me to the core to see her mouth as she bravely slurped at the head of each crawfish. She sucked at the brains of every single craw-skull with such sensuality and native zeal that I felt feverish. I watched only her: she tossed aside the corpses and swigged beer and laughed gaily. Someone called my name: someone shouted it: but I ignored the voices. I slid my hand down under my apron, inside my checkered pants and walked, in a sexual trance, back into the dining room.

I stood at her side once again, holding a crawfish in my free hand. I held it over her, then up against her lips. At first she looked amused, unaware that my reappearance was decidedly more passionate. When she noticed the placement of my other hand she became alarmed, shook her head and pushed me away. Rough hands grabbed my arms and dragged me away from the table. As I was yanked away from her I admired the stains on her blouse, saw the hot-sauce dribbling down her chin as she gaped in horror. I flew backward through the diningroom and away from my beloved starlet. I felt my back smash painfully against a swinging door as it hit me coming the wrong way through it.

I found myself on the ground in the back courtyard of the Bistro de. The stink of garbage was sharp enough to revive me from temporary unconsciousness. Damp and dark and chilling, the courtyard filled with sudden light as someone opened the kitchen door wide. A pail of crawfish carcasses was tossed out over me, followed by my jacket.

As far as I was concerned, it was a case of unappreciated zeal.

I moved around the country a great deal after the crawfish incident. Getting work was difficult because employers wanted references. I could only work where none were required. The incidents, however, became more frequent. In Santa Fe I was fired for trying to climb onto the laps of a couple who were feeding each other kalamari. It became so hard for me to find a job that I ended up working the rib-and-chicken circuit all the way down to Texas. Texas is where I met my end. I tried to kiss a Baptist minister while he was eating fried chicken I'd prepared, tried to stick my tongue in his mouth while he was chewing. It was he who insisted I be put away. I wonder now: if I had waited until he finished chewing and swallowed if he would have been more receptive to my attentions? Religious leaders can be quite testy about having their meals interrupted...

Anyway, the newspapers got wind of the scandal and I've been here in this hospital for quite awhile. They've forced me to hang up my cheffy-whites for an indefinite period. I have to stay here until I admit that I am ill, but I won't admit anything of the sort! I keep my chef's hat hidden under the bed and take it out at night. I wear it until the morning nurse comes and tries to confiscate it. She calls it an unhealthy prop that is interfering with my ability to get well. But the nurse can be bought. I can usually talk her into letting me keep it with the revelations of a few secret recipes. She's writing a cookbook in her spare time and knows I was once a great chef before passion destroyed my psyche.

I still *love* food; passionately and too much. The doctors say they can cure me of this love. Cure me by turning me into their very own clinical crawfish: they suck the juice from my brain with talk and medication, then toss me back onto my bed of newspapers when they've finished with me. When I tell them I love cooking more than sex they simply nod and smile. Watching people eat thrills my soul. Without that thrill I am spiritually starved! Apparently spiritual nourishment is of no importance here. Satisfaction can't be measured by their machines.

They want to know what it is exactly that excites me about watching people eat. One doctor follows me around the cafeteria with a clipboard and notes my responses. I tell him that he is wasting his time: if I haven't cooked the food myself it has no effect on me. This is very interesting to the doctors, but they still want me to explain why the connection between cooking and watching people eat is an erotic one for me.

"Mothers breastfeed. Watch their faces. They get *turned on*. Why don't you put all of the mothers in this world away in mental hospitals, too?"

They tell me quickly that the disturbed longings I experience can hardly be compared to the natural maternal stimulation felt by nursing mothers.

"What's the first thing we learn to do in this world? We learn to *suck*. When people eat they suck and chew and devour. They repeat the first delight of existence each time they eat! I find that thrilling," I say.

"But your position is neither infantile nor maternal. Yours is a voyeuristic pleasure—er—disorder. You become inappropriately excited by watching people eat food you have prepared. Your lack of sexual control makes your neurosis distinctly different from maternal pleasure. Let's be absolutely clear about that." My psychiatrist is obviously pleased by his own vocabulary. He smiles to himself.

I ask him if he was breastfed. He blushes scarlet and his smile disappears. He asks me quietly if I have ever experienced any disturbances in my eating habits, any disorders.

"No, no eating disorders," I say, "but apparently I have a cooking disorder." When he glares at me over his spectacles, I continue, "I have no problem with food. I like to cook. And watching people eat the food I cook gets me horny. Where's the problem in that?"

He sighs, "The *behaviour* is the problem, not the impulse. I am trying to help you understand where the impulse is coming from so that you can learn to keep it from resulting in action." He pushes his glasses down to the end of his nose and peers intently at his notepad. "Perhaps you are struggling with your own desire to give birth, to breastfeed. You may be having difficulty directing this desire toward the selection of a mate. We have noted that you exhibit no sexual preference when approaching diners. The desire you are experiencing is becoming misdirected in your psyche and may now be desribed as a neurotic problem." He looks very pleased with himself all of a sudden.

I lean very far forward in my chair and tell him that a degree in psychology must be worth very little. That if the world is full of hungry people and those who enjoy feeding them are persecuted, then the concept of mental health is a dubious yardstick. The doctor begins to interrupt with a speech on messiah complexes and I yawn loudly to show my disdain. Our session is terminated for the day.

A few days later my shrink and I are walking in the yard outside the hospital and he sees a girl sitting on the hood of a car eating an ice-cream cone. Though he struggles to pay attention to what I am saying he is distracted. His eyes drift back to the girl several times.

"Food and sex have no natural connection, Doctor," I say, shaking my finger at him. He begins walking in the opposite direction, away from the girl, and I can see his ears going crimson.

I am discharged from the hospital two days later. The doctor and I discuss my condition one last time. I must try to control my behaviour. Thoughts are of no danger if I don't allow them to lead to action. I will be able to cook again! My greatest passion in life is cooking and I never want to lose that pleasure again. On my way home from the hospital I stop at Woolworth's. The doctor has prescribed lollipops as a form of treatment. When I am back working in a kitchen again I will take my bag of lollipops with me and keep them handy at all times. That way, if I catch a glimpse of people eating in the dining room, I can curb my desires by sucking at one of these sweets.

My shrink told me he once used this method of treatment on himself and it worked. I guess I'll just have to test it out. I have an interview at a restaurant next week, an appointment set up for me by the kind nurse at the hospital. I'm very excited. It's an open-kitchen concept where you can see the customers eating and they can see you cooking. I know for a fact that there are people out there who find watching cooks cooking *very* exciting...

Mamamilk

The sorrow of the river makes even the best of Mamas take a cocktail to bed. Trip upstairs to the sheets with a jangling cup of scotch, the night crushing in on her shoulders. Some man may have wandered off, leaving the mother to love a baby, or babies. Who knows how many mistakes love has made with each Mama? And so a Mama goes to bed, alone and looking forward to the relief of a scotchy, beautiful slumber; to a dead-drunk doze.

One Mama in New Orleans pushed her first little boy off the G.N. Wharf. No one saw, and even later, in a drunken stupor, she never told a soul. Few people ever knew about the child. He had gone right under, obediently and without so much as a scream, and left her to her life as though he'd never been part of its pain.

Not two years later, up bobbed a second little boy, the fruit of another weak time when her dreams of love got the best of her. She let another handsome grin talk her into motherhood; let the warmth of a pair of hands push her into something. A second little baby boy came along and the warm pair of hands fluttered away soon after. She loved the little boy as best she could; impatiently, angrily, but with a generous, nervous love.

He grew quickly, out of his clothes like a wild weed, punishing her wallet with his stretching limbs. It was probably a punishment from God, for pushing the first little boy into the Mississippi. She thought this every time she looked at her second son. He grew too fast, ate too much. She perceived it as a lesson life was trying to teach her. A hard lesson, a punch-in-the-guts parable that she went over and over in her head at night. The more she tried to figure out what life was trying to teach her, the more glasses of scotch she would take up to bed with her. She knew she had it in her to be a good Mama to someone. She would work it out between sips.

By the time the little boy was twelve, she was carrying a tray-full of spilling tumblers up the stairs to her bed. Her night-table was covered with sticky empty glasses every morning, her head rocked on her shoulders. To rouse her, the little boy banged one of the tumblers on the headboard of her bed. He stood above her, the tallest little boy she had ever seen, and grinned his mean grin. He sat across from her at breakfast and fixed his angry gaze on her, scraping his spoon to annoy her. He shouted for more cereal when he knew the box was empty.

The more she looked at him, the more she thought of throwing herself into the Mississippi. She thought about it every afternoon while he was in school. She wrote long poems about desire and instead of jumping into the river, threw the poems into the water and walked slowly along the bank until the paper went under. It gave her a deep feeling of satisfaction to watch the beautiful white pages sink into the churning brown. She wondered if maybe her other little boy was somewhere down-river, catching the poems and reading them. The idea of him sitting on a log, reading her sad, wandering, too-long poems gave her comfort. He would know from the poems that she felt bad about what she'd done to him. That she hadn't meant to push him so roughly. He'd been such a good boy, sunk so quickly.

Sometimes she tried to go up to her bedroom without a drink. To sleep without the assistance of liquor. Her young son stayed out late sometimes, too late for a boy his age. On those nights she wanted to be a good mother, wait up and scold him, express her worry. She sat on the edge of the bed with her fists clenched, listening hard for the whine of the screendoor. After a few hours, straining to hear, she gave up the façade. She wasn't worried at all, and could not pretend to be. Somewhere, deep in her soul, she wished something would happen to the boy. That she could be alone again.

She dreamt that she was breastfeeding him, but he was a grown boy. He spat out her nipple. He spat and spat, and an endless flow of breast-milk and mud-water flowed from her teat. He swore at her and sneered with disgust. When she slapped him, her hand went right through him.

An endless chain of mornings and nights led her to believe that she would never see her son again. He did not come home late, or at all, and she did not call the police or ask the neighbours if they had seen him around town. She kept to her bedroom, going down to the kitchen to fetch fresh trays of glasses. She never brought the bottle of scotch upstairs with her. To her that represented complete gluttony, and southern women were never gluttons. Instead she filled several small glasses and drank that way, slowly and heavily.

It gave her such relief to know that he had gone for good. She woke up one afternoon knowing that he would not return. She guessed that a young boy like him could be ready for the world. She supposed he'd gone out looking for the part of the world he could stand to live in. She hoped it was far away, but she couldn't be sure he would ever leave New Orleans.

For the longest time she was smart about love. She kept it away from her and spent most of her nights at home. The only males she saw were the Verti-Mart delivery boys who brought her scotch on their bicycles. None of them were interested in love, only in gratuities. It suited her fine: she ordered, she waited, and they brought her three big bottles of scotch and a tub of potato salad. She ate the salad all week. It was the only food that appealed to her. It gave her just enough energy to climb up and down the stairs, but not enough to make her want to leave the house.

When it rained she thought a great deal about her two lost sons. The one in the river seemed more precious and real, the one who had fled seemed like a ghost. She drank her way through the frequent thunderstorms of the Louisiana summer and wrote poems about bloody murder to make herself sick at heart. She knew she was a terrible mother, but she began to think about having another child. She refused to ever have another child out of imagined love. That was over: she could not be fooled again. She was smart now and could finally be the good Mama she dreamt of being.

When the Verti-Mart boy rode up on his bicycle she wore perfume and her old kimono. She pretended to read a book of poems and watched him struggle with the canvas sack full of bottles. He cursed to himself and she decided he was perfect: angry, naive, and completely unattractive.

He climbed on top of her on the kitchen table and it had nothing to do with love. She requested, he obliged, and it was over within minutes. It reminded her that life could be simple if a person insisted on simplicity. When she went to bed that night with only one glass of scotch, she felt her life improving in small ways.

Again she gave birth to a little boy. This time she decided not to hide herself away in the house like a fallen woman. She bought a stroller for the baby and went for long, long walks. They paraded up and down Decatur Street, stopping from time to time at various bars along the way. She began to buy her groceries at the Verti-Mart shop instead of having them delivered. The women who ran the shop were not nearly as pleasant as the delivery boys. They disapproved of her, she could see that. Still, she did as she pleased: paraded her little boy around, had a few cocktails. She made a lot of new friends in the cool, dark bars.

A happy Mama makes for a happy baby.

It must have been true, because the longer she sat and talked with her new friends, the quieter the baby was. When they went back out into the bright sunlight, he never cried. He must've known how happy his Mama was. They walked all over the Quarter every single day, and there was always a little money. Men liked to give her a few dollars. They told her to buy her little son a present or two, buy herself something. All she had to do was sit and talk with them and let them light her cigarettes. They wanted so little, bought so many drinks. Besides, a hand on a thigh was not Love.

Occasionally, when they walked home after a long day of visiting her friends in the bars, she stumbled. The street names confused her. The cobblestones bit at her high-heels. If she fell to the ground, passersby clucked their tongues in vague disgust. The police never interfered. She was his Mama, she could raise him as she pleased. It did-n't matter to the police that the little boy was too big for his stroller. Was too old for it, after a time. His shoes dragged along the sidewalk all the way home, each and every evening. She didn't notice: she was happy.

Sometimes the men in the bars tried to convince her to let the little boy run around a bit. She refused to let him out of the stroller when they were out. He was too wild, she said. He liked to just sit, she insisted upon it. No amount of urging could make her let him out of that stroller. She was his Mama, after all.

* * *

The little boy was almost five. He was very quiet. He threw his toys to the floor and frowned. It upset the other people in the bar when she shrieked at him to be quiet when he had barely uttered a word. Strangers decided that she was a very bad mother. At one time it had been amusing to her friends that she took him to bars. His misery had not been quite so obvious then.

One Thursday she wanted to have a cocktail away from the usual crowd. She wandered into a new place, a side-street bar. The little boy was, as usual, jammed into the confines of the stroller. Cigarette ashes fell on him from her left hand as she pushed the stroller and smoked. Watery scotch splashed onto his arms from the plastic cup she held in her right hand. In her effort to navigate the stroller through the narrow doorway, she spilled a great deal of scotch. The bartender watched her entrance and shook his head. There she was, smoking and splashing, not a care in the world for her little boy. The bartender was very familiar with her famous promenades.

She left the little boy strapped into the stroller and rolled him over to the jukebox. She imagined that he enjoyed the flashing lights and loud bursts of music and took a seat at the bar.

"J.B. 'n rocks, please," she said. The bartender watched her light a cigarette. He set the drink down in front of her and she emptied it. "'Nother one," she sighed, blowing smoke out between clenched teeth.

"Trying to forget something?" the bartender asked casually. He served her a generous double that she didn't even acknowledge. When she grunted in reply he giggled to himself. He tried again, "Is that your new baby?"

"*New* baby? He's my *only* baby." She laughed nervously.

"Is that so?" he asked, half to himself, but she heard him.

"That is so," she said flatly, looking at the bartender through narrowed eyes. There was no reason to continue making small-talk with him. He was young and handsome, but he gave her the creeps with his staring eyes and bitter smile. To prove that he could not get to her with his odd comments, she remained seated. He offfered to buy her a drink and she became suspicious.

"It's my birthday, have one with me," he smiled.

"Do you have any idea how many men use that line?"

"But it really is my birthday. July twelfth. July the twelfth. C'mon, mama, have a drink with me!"

"Don't call me Mama, okay? I'll have one."

He poured out two large shots and a cup of orange juice for the little boy. Seeing the juice, she grudgingly climbed down from the stool and took it over to her son. He could barely hold a cup and spilled most of it on himself. He began to wimper but she was already back in her seat at the bar, eager for her own free drink.

The bartender held up a glass and she did the same, amused by his drama. He wasn't bad looking, a bit of a creep. But a generous creep could always be tolerated, for a time. He swirled the scotch around in his glass and winked at her, and something in his face looked so familiar that she shuddered. He held the drink up to the light and then downed it, shouting, "Ahhh! Mamamilk!"

"Happy Birthday, asshole," she nodded, downing her own.

"You've always been such a sentimental gal, haven't you?" His eyes were cold and fixed on hers. "I hope your new little boy can swim as well as the others."

She felt the sudden need to get the hell out of that bar. She did not look up from her purse as she fished frantically for cigarettes. He kept his eyes on her but she would not look up. It was a miracle that she managed to climb down off the barstool. Her legs trembled as she went to the stroller and yanked it out of the bar. On her way, she smashed into several chairs, the doorframe. The sun blinded her and she stumbled down Royal Street, the little boy screaming all the way. Somehow she found their street, got back to the house.

Safe inside, she left her screaming son in the dark living room, still strapped into the stroller. She went into the kitchen. Standing over the sink, she drank the last of the scotch she had; straight from the bottle, no glass, no tray. She sank to the floor and sat listening to her little boy's screams of frustration. She knew them well, and joined in.

Belly

Tomorrow's Home Owner's Pride Day. They've proclaimed it a national Festival Day and parades are popping up in all major cities and modest towns. Scarlet banners fly and the grinning property owners wear bright t-shirts screened with renderings of their personal castles. Owning a home has become such a thing-unique that people feel the need to shout about it. It's the stroll of the chosen few bringing in the slain unicorn. I haven't seen a house I could capture in two decades, but this is the *third annual* parade.

I'm holding a brunch in honour of my lucky friends, the ones with two-car garages and split-level lives. Known them all since university. Even the single woman among them managed to get her teeth into a pill-box townhouse in the suburbs. And is she *happy!* She's glad and she'll tell you just how. In between arguing with fellow home-owners about Euro-style kitchen fixtures. She doesn't even have to *say* you see, her hands move like she *owns* something.

My friends were told I've got a luxury condo downtown with a solarium, central air and vac, a distant view of some water. And it's right on *the Parade route!* I am some kind of urbanite success! Even if it is only a *condo*, I know that's what they mutter to each other. They have their very own squares of grass on which their dogs can piss and pant. They can watch the urination ceremony from a freshly stained deck. No, I wasn't aware of the gratification involved in owning a shrub and seeing it pissed on, but apparently it's immense.

They've lost track of exactly where it is I live: I moved so many times before finding the *condo*. The only time I call these friends of mine is when I move, to let them know my new telephone number. It was my fate to be pencilled into people's address books. One of the guys I've invited to brunch today took to calling me his *gypsy friend* with a kind of cozier-than-thou tone in his voice. I invited him to brunch first. He rents rooms to IBM execs. The ones who prefer owning a BMW to owning a mortgage. He describes them as having *no priority system*. Their lack of castle-lust is laughable to him. I think I'll seat him next to me at this soiree.

I think I bragged of serving Cornish game hens and salmon mousse. They all seemed mildly excited by the prospect of seeing where it is that I live *and* eat so well. I mentioned Beaujolais and track-lighting. A solarium packed with telescopes and other toys I know they covet. Remote everything, mod cons of all types. I know this brunch will make it all worthwhile, because reality dictates that my friends will be a little surprised by what I call a *condo*.

I step out of my shower (tubless): I'm in my living room: bedroom: kitchen. I clear away the stacks of Real Estate News from the sofa (bed, rarely folded into sofa position unless it's absolutely necessary: today it is) and sit where I can prop my feet on the half-fridge and cut my toenails.

My feet, in fact, are resting on Brunch. The fridge is full of those hot-plate-simple frozen boxes plastered with bright orange stickers: 79. I only shop when I absolutely *have* to eat. Nights when I'm not at my second job, when my stomach sizzles with neglect, I nibble. Usually I just bring home the Real Estate papers and roll pennies while I read. Today I care less about the needs of my stomach and more for the honour of my Houseproud friends.

I've told them all to come at different times. Staggered the starting-time for our party to cater to their individual tendencies toward lateness, promptness, prematurity. It is important that they all land at the door at the same time. One guy is always late because his mortgage payments mean he's been driving the same car for nine years. He'll drive it into the ground, he jokes. Or an early grave. The woman is always early. She imagines the suburbs are so much further away from the downtown core than they actually are. She *can't believe* that she has a backyard *and* access to cultural diversity, should she choose to want it.

Will they gather together in the dark foyer and wonder what the joke is? See the security code board ripped from the wall by unfriendly neighbours and the mailboxes charred by a recent fire? Worry about the smell of fried chicken clinging to their cashmere? I head up the narrow stairs between hunched slabs of drywall. I live in what's called the Second Basement, a dug-out addition to this renovated once-house. I hear an orchestra of other people's TVs, someone shouting that they're too tired to fight about "it" anymore. Then I see Alice, touching her hair in confusion while William and Brandon clutch at their glossy gift-bags of house-warming wine. They all look freshly laundered, being Maytag owners, and all three wear horrified smiles.

I'm bright, I'm casual, I'm the perfect host.

"Come on in," I beam, taking arms and nudging shoulders. "Watch your head there, Brandon."

Uncomfortable chuckles. "What's this? A royal tour of local historical ruins?" William jokes, hugging his wine-bag.

I lead them down the stairs to my door. I turn a key in the lock of my home, 2B-7. Pushing them all inside, I slam the freshly painted fire-proof door. Alice is sniffing for Cornish hens, William is looking for the solarium. I take coats, hang them on the shower head. Seat the guests: two on the sofa, one on a card-chair.

"Sooo," I smile. I'm really enjoying watching the colour drain from their faces. I explain about not having enough room in the fridge for their wine just yet, but that after Brunch I'll chill it right up.

Do I mind if they smoke?

"Hell no, the central air'll suck it right up. Anyone want a drink?"

There is unanimous acceptance of my offer. We drink warm wine for this house-warming. I pour myself a glass first, drink it down, then pour theirs. After all, it's my home. Their disgust makes me giddy. They'll soon whip out their Law and Psych degrees for an interrogation. Get to the bottom of this impractical joke. But it's my gala, and I'll run it. I'm supposed to be honouring them, and I am, in my way. They want more drinks, I provide. I'm a superior host. I serve and chat with wit and ease. I make tender inquiries about lawncare, satellite dishes, termite statistics. I slowly squeeze the pleasure from their usual obsessive topics. Interlocking bricktalk is no longer orgasmic for William.

I hold the meal off for as long as I can. I want them to really *know* hunger. I pretend to need to know just *how much* blood-and-bone-meal is good for the flower-beds. My own hunger may interfere with my mission; I notice that my hands are shaking more than usual. But I'm counting on my stamina when it comes to an empty belly. I force myself not to think about eating and instead mention the increase in parasites gnawing away at our public parks. I ask if any of them have ever encountered a rabid squirrel on their *own* property?

Brandon and William both want to use the toilet. I wave my hand over my shoulder, "Where the coats are. But one at a time, please. The second bathroom's under renovation." I turn to Alice and, in a confidential tone, whisper, "The jacuzzi, you know." She tries to pretend she doesn't hear William performing his bodily functions.

"Great accoustics in here," I nod. "Too bad I'm not a musician."

They reassemble, filling the ashtrays I've set out for them: tuna cans with the labels washed off. I don't empty the ashtrays, figuring they like accumulating things. My questions are met with pale smiles, not replies. I decide that it's time for food.

"Brunch?"

Alice nods like a maniac. Wine seems to transform her into a rubber dolly with eyes red and blinking from the cigarettes she rarely smokes. Cigarettes stain the broadloom in her world. She never did have the courage to abuse herself with any kind of conviction.

I put on an apron. Brandon gives in and heads for the toilet. The stack of frozen turkey pies startles Alice and William. I think they look lovely, the pies, all frost-kissed, like in the commercials. I remember watching TV, watching it until it dawned on me that all TV commercials are set in *homes*. The happy sitcoms, too. I gave my TV away to a nursing home right after that epiphany.

"Need help?" There's Alice, anchoring herself in domesticity. She leans forward on her chair and a rough edge cuts into her pantyhose. I like her wince, it's so... settled.

"No, no, no. Just sit tight. Enjoy yourself. I just have to chop these up and the hardest part's over. Are you all as hungry as I am? Some days I worry about myself, I get so ravenous!"

I hack the pies into shards, roll them in margarine, plug in the electric skillet. With my free hand I pour them more wine. Cold boxed wine I've been saving for a celebration. I think of a toast and raise my cup:

"To my friends, who *glow* with ownership."

The fridge door is ajar and my pistol falls out onto the floor. I've been keeping it cold, planning to show it to them when their mouths were full. But it's out in full view now. I point it fast at Alice's head.

William is up, he's fatherly. "OK, OK, joke's over." But he stays near the sofa. His fingers, spread in alarm, are white and his smiling lips are dry.

They give me the "Hey, what's with you?" and the "Such a joker!" They talk to me as though we're all back in university.

Behind me the turkey is burning and they want me to notice it. It's the sickening smell of blackening bubbling gravy and coagulated carrots. I keep the gun on them and scoop them each a heaping plateful. I refill their glasses. Now they take microscopic sips of wine and fear the food.

Brandon's mad between mouthfuls. "What the hell is this all about?" He's the one with the most to lose, having just installed a sauna and kidney-shaped swimming pool *inside* his house. He's also got a lot of unused travel points built up. Things to live for.

William speaks softly, "What about the condo?"

Some people's politesse near death.

"Did something *bad* happen to you?" Alice wants.

I tip the gun toward the ceiling, chewing slowly. "No, nothing bad, Alice. Only *good* things come my way. My life is one long romantic walk, one long romantic line-up. I lined up to live here, for example. And in the several dozen banks where I've been turned down by loan officers, I lined up. Those banklines are like breadlines to the hungry, the *house*-hungry. And the Bank," I point the gun at a jar of pennies near Brandon's foot, "the Bank is a soup-kitchen. Big pots of money boil on the shelves, just out of reach. And the people who hold the ladles can read our faces and see that we're beyond desperate, willing to tell lies, fudge figures. And they slap our hands and tell us to seek the help of our parents. But our parents are basically *dead*, you see, from working to pay for our educations. Our parents have nothing left to give, and they didn't expect to have to, since the equation was always Big Education means Big Job means at least, a Small Bungalow."

Alice realizes that the backyard she worships could be cited as her Cause of Death.

"I talked to a lot of people in those line-ups because I had the time. And I figured that if I was courteous and friendly and twice-as-frugal with *my* pennies, that someone would give me a break. That I would charm my chances for a loan."

I see them in their damp expensive clothes rented from VISA and snicker. They try to look sympathetic but it's a life they just don't believe can happen. They are all Real Successful Human Beings. The nursery rooms are empty and waiting. I happen to know that Alice is three months pregnant. I take the gun and press it up against her womb.

"ENOUGH!" William shouts. From the sofa. Always a man for safe distances. As though security can be found in furniture.

"I wouldn't," I whisper. "I want you and the Little One to march in that Parade tomorrow, Alice. But I want you to think about what that Little One can look forward to. Don't be so sure about what the world has to offer.

Anyway, my gun is too warm. I like to use it when it's nice and cold." I move to put the gun back in the fridge.

I keep them there on the sofa and chair for hours, my feet propped on the fridge where it's comfortable to watch them. No one sleeps. The light in the room never changes as night turns into morning: there are no windows in the Second Basement. The room is rank with sweat and worry. The Parade will begin soon. None of them have their special t-shirts or banners.

"Time to march!" I say. My voice scares them. I take the gun out of the fridge and feel in cold in my palm, frosty as an after-work beer.

William looks at me, beard darkening to a shadow on his jaw. "You don't *have* to live this way," he grunts. "I've seen your other apartments. Nice places. Clean. This isn't healthy, and it's not about money. I know you have the *cash* to live normally." He waits for me to answer. "Don't you?"

I move them out into the hall at gunpoint. They all look exhausted, having smoked too much and slept too little. And the turkey pies *were* slightly past their best-before dates.

"Is this about drugs?" Alice asks gently. She needs an answer, believes in them.

"*Go* to the Parade. I hear there are two new home-owners this year. They'll give them medallions on the platform. Drink lemonade, toast them in the sunshine." All three of my friends smile, touching their shirts at their collars. Their own medallions are hidden by their clothes, but the mere touch through fabric reminds them of their financial glory. It lets them know how special they are.

I close the door against their feeble suggestions that I join them, come along to see what's possible.

My clock says it's one p.m. I plug my phone back into the wall and it rings almost immediately. It's a woman I met recently in one of the many bank line-ups. She's a school-teacher, single. She just found out she's been turned down again by yet another bank. Still ten thousand short, even after a month of moonlighting as a prostitute. She tries not to cry into the phone. I remind her of the Parade that's going on for us, too. She says she thinks it's the best solution. I agree with her and hang up. We have to wait until one thirty-five p.m.

While I wait I hear the distant honks of cars and the cheers of the Homeowner's Pride Parade crowd. For a brief moment my optimism is seduced. Good things. To those who wait... but no. I, too have Pride. I've waited and waited. I lift the gun to my head and join the private Parade of thousands of people just like me. People who have silently decided, packed into fire-trap apartments, hotels and hostels; the couples in basements jammed with rented furniture and skinny kids... We've all made a pact, one arranged in bank line-ups across the country. We'll march, and we'll make a big, angry bang as we go, eating cake and bullets.

The Motel Joneses

Soon after their wedding day, Fred and Glenda Jones knew trouble was upon them. In the *sex* department, anyway. Everything else was rosy-red marital peaches and cream. They had *stuff:* a car, a bungalow, and parents cheering them on from both sides.

Because their relationship began as an illicit affair, their pre-marital relations involved a great deal of sneaking around. They often found themselves in by-the-hour highway motor-inns, of necessity. But it was all somehow titillating. He could get it up, she could scream like a Hallowe'en witch. Though furtive and clandestine, things had been great in the sex department.

Then there were churchbells, presents, fists full of rice. There was the traditional gluttonous reception and a night of hump-and-bump in a downtown Holiday Inn. The planets were properly aligned and the Law had given the nod; they were married at last, freed from their previous marriages by quick visits to lawyers. Each had been married to a less passionate partner, and Fred and Glenda were thrilled to be safe in each other's spirited arms. 'Til Death blew her whistle, forever and ever! It seemed that their hunger for each other would never wane. And so they married.

At first they couldn't understand what was wrong. On their first official night of cozy-in-the-bungalow there seemed to be a mutual case of nuptial bad nerves. They hit the lights and called it quits, cuddling instead. They were exhausted: left weak from the endless wedding arrangements: the fittings, the hirings and firings of numerous caterers, the things necessary to any good wedding's execution.

As time went on and Fred was promoted at work, they decided to blame their lacking lust on Fred's handsomely paying job. Glenda was dutifully respectful of her husband's draining responsibilities. She read books about lighting his fire and took some courses in massage. A good rub-down was supposed to crank him up, but his passionate snoring after fifteen minutes of oily paw-work on her part proved the massage manuals wrong. Glenda watched talk shows and learned that she was to blame, though Fred tried to tell her it just wasn't her fault.

Fred and Glenda Jones had been raised right. She asked her mother for advice and he had a few beers with his wise old dad. Glenda's mom couldn't believe that the massages hadn't worked, because they still seemed to get Glenda's father stirred up. Fred's dad was a little more philosophical about the problem and suggested some S/M games. A little role playing would surely do the trick.

Standing at the end of the dining room table in his zipper-hood and chains, with his darling Glenda strapped down and immobile, Fred wasn't sure they had chosen the right costumes. When he couldn't manage to hang onto the cattle-prod because of his sweaty palms, he untied Glenda and they sat, rubberclad and miserable on the sofa, eating Cantonese food.

It looked like counselling was the only option. Since the day after their honeymoon night at the Holiday Inn, neither Fred nor Glenda had been coitally satisfied. There had been plenty of solo-induced shivering, but marriage wasn't about endless bathroom privacy. Marriage was obviously about counselling.

In the Spice House

Dr. Annette sat across from the Joneses in her plant-filled office. She asked them questions about Moms and Dads. She inquired about their sex lives before they met. Had they tried touch-therapy? Had they explored the possibilities of sensual massage? When Glenda burst into tears at the mention of aromatherapy, Annette decided the problem was more complicated than she had suspected.

"How did the two of you meet and *connect?*" Dr. Annette asked.

"We were both involved with other people," Fred began.

Annette sat forward in her easychair and stopped playing with her pen for the first time during the session. Fred stared back at her, expecting an explanation. After staring at the Joneses for several moments, she finally said, "Sounds like intimacy issues." She beamed proudly and pressed her fingertips together.

"Not enough intimacy?" Glenda piped in, curious, because she had heard about intimacy.

Annette shook her head, "Too much!"

"Sounds like you need to book a room at the Motel Six, buddy," Fred's best friend Loomis said, that same evening over drinks. Loomis had been hearing about Fred's affair with Glenda since their very first tryst. He felt very connected to the couple, and had no patience for therapists, having been in therapy himself for eight and a half years.

"What's Motel Six got to do with intimacy issues?" Fred cried out, at the end of his sexual rope.

"This isn't about intimacy, Freddy. It's about miniature bars of soap, and free movies, and menacing chambermaids. It's about setting the scene. Get me?"

By the end of the night Loomis had convinced Fred that all the Joneses needed was a night in a motel room to reignite their former flame. He called up the local Motel

Six and booked his friend and his bride a bargain-rate room with a parking-lot view.

And, on the very next night, nervous and desperate, Fred and Glenda Jones pulled into the Motel Six parking lot with nothing but a shaving kit and Glenda's diaphragm-jelly love-pack. The man at the front desk took down the information, a faint glow in his goiterish eyes.

"You kids be good now," he called after them, returning with disinterest to his copy of Kinderlust magazine. The photos of grown women dressed as dollies just didn't do it for him anymore...

Fred fumbled with the key and Glenda hummed under her breath. Yet it was like a fantasy coming true when Fred pushed the door wide open. A waft of motel carpet hit them both square on. They looked at each other with ardent eyes and shoved into the room simultaneously.

Glenda could smell the rubber backing on the daisy-spattered curtains. She moved to the light switch with a pounding heart, drunk on the smell of Gideon Bibles and paper-wrapped drinking glasses.

"You want a rye?" Fred asked, his back to Glenda. He'd brought a bottle along in case they ended up chatting.

When Fred glanced up into the bureau mirror he saw his beloved Glenda stretched out and hungry on the crushed velvet bedspread with a look of thrilled passion lighting her face.

"Here kitty-kitty," Glenda growled, in a voice Fred had almost forgotten.

The Joneses were at long last keeping up with themselves.

When morning came and a chambermaid stuck her unwelcome key in the lock, Fred was mid-yelp for the seventh time and Glenda was using words like "Ride!" and "Go!" Without missing a beat Fred told the maid to go straight to hell and the Joneses went spiralling into their favourite place in the heavens.

"Loomis, you're my saviour," Fred chuckled into the phone the next Monday morning. He was smiling to himself as he hung up and dialed the number of Flora-Belle's to order daisies for Glenda.

The card read, "Like the daisies on the curtains at Motel Six."

The Joneses have been together for years and years. On their anniversary they send Loomis a card of thanks. Their accountant can't believe the money they spend on weekend getaways, but Fred insists the jaunts are necessary expenses and won't cut back. Friday nights the Joneses hop in their car and drive to towns a few hours away, trying new motels and hotels and triple-tiered motor-inns. In between trips the Joneses jones, dreaming of the things they will do to each other with small bars of soap and scratchy white towels.

The Joneses felt it only proper to have some kids along the way. Three times the diaphragm-jelly love-pack was left at home in a kind of oops-we-forgot, aren't-we-naughty spirit. The results of their occasional amnesia have been three lovely daughters: Delta, Chelsea, and Holiday-Ann.

The Butcher Loves The Baker

The butcher loves the baker but the baker can't, or won't, love the butcher back. Though the butcher adores the way the baker muscles bread, the baker is not mutually impressed by the butcher's techniques, and so remains cold; though she was once oven-warm for a sprinkle of minutes.

The butcher first saw the baker as a celebrity, displayed in the window of the Les Affaires Bakery on Boule Saint-Laurent. The baker made a grand showpiece for the bakery: she was a striking brunette and looked strong as she loaded bagels into the fiery mouth of the brick oven. At first the butcher simply admired the baker through glass. When she was sure she could guarantee her own poise, the butcher stepped into the coziness of the Les Affaires and watched the baker from her place in line. She began to shop there and abandoned her love of Wonderbread in hopes of one day meeting the baker. The baker was cordoned off by counters like a sacred craftsgal and it was a challenge to get her attention, but the butcher was determined.

She was tenacious and haunted the shop, convinced by her first glimpse of the baker that they were meant to meet and know each other well. It was powerful, that first and sudden sighting of the baker after years of strolling down Saint-Laurent. And so, with her usual good-natured grace, the butcher frequented the bakery until circumstances allowed them to meet.

The Les Affaires had a young cashier who was miserably slow. On one particularly busy afternoon the baker took over the register in an effort to erode the growing line-up at the counter. Though she was officially off-duty and had finished her turn at the oven, she volunteered her services in the name of Good Business. The line-up soon dwindled to a trio of people: a plumber, a doctor, and the heartsick butcher.

When it was the butcher's turn to request her bagels, she knew it was a moment arranged by the cosmos, and one to be seized. Though her small freezer at home was already stuffed with uneaten bagels, she ordered two-dozen poppy-seeds in an effort to seem grand. The baker smiled warmly at the butcher and seemed to take extra care in bagging her bagels.

"I guess you like bagels," the baker said. "You buy so many."

"I buy them for friends," said the butcher, desperate to find a way to introduce herself.

"But you must live close by. You're here so often."

The butcher nodded, "Very nearby."

The baker charged the butcher for one dozen bagels instead of two and it was Fate, pushing the butcher to do something, because one rarely gets such a bargain for no reason at all. But the butcher, who spent her days chopping carcasses, was terribly timid, and could find nothing to say.

The baker, who looked absolutely charming with bits of baguette in her hair, leaned over the counter and stared at the butcher as though expecting something. When the butcher remained silent, the baker sighed, and shrugged as though defeated.

"Have a nice day!" the baker called out, heading for the coatrack near the oven. The butcher could not move to leave, nor could she find her voice, and her face turned scarlet as she stood there helplessly. The baker was dressing to leave.

Outside the Les Affaires the wind was sharp, and the butcher tugged at her scarf. She stood away from the window and nervously clutched her bag of bagels. When the baker emerged from the shop, the butcher called out to her and smiled.

"Hello? Would you like to have coffee?"

The baker laughed and said, "I would. I know a good place where they won't make you eat any more bagels. I promise."

The butcher and baker walked to a quiet café a few blocks away. As it turned out, it was a place they both knew. The woman who ran the café was a good friend of the baker's and a casual acquaintance to the butcher. When they entered the café the woman looked surprised to see them together but said nothing except hello. She brought them coffee and hurried away. They sat across from each other and grinned like fools, stirring their black coffees. Finally they began to talk and laugh and actually drink from their cups. Both were distracted from the conversation by thoughts of how to get the other back to her apartment. Their attraction to one another was almost embarrassing for the woman running the café. She hoped they would leave and not order more coffee.

The butcher called out to her, "Madge, could you bring us some more coffee when you have time?" She could not take her eyes off the baker, and if they weren't going to go home to bed together, she wanted to stare at the baker for as long as she could.

The baker marveled at the beautiful strong hands of her coffee companion. She tore her lustful eyes away from the butcher's strong fingers and looked up to find her smiling nervously.

"What do you do for a living?" the baker asked. "Are you a sculptor?"

"I'm a butcher," the butcher said proudly. It was a non-traditional field, after all.

You could ask the butcher today what happened next but she wouldn't be able to recall the exact sequence of events. Just seconds after she revealed her profession, the baker vomited violently into her coffee cup and emitted a series of disgusted howls. The owner of the café rushed over with a towel, but reached the table just as it went over on its side. The baker was flinging furniture and cutlery and Sweet 'n Low packets everywhere a fit of rage.

"My God! What's wrong?" the butcher shouted, dodging saucers and flying miniature buckets of cream.

Madge pulled the butcher out of the line of fire and handed her the towel to wipe herself off with. The baker was somewhat quieter and now regarded the butcher with wild eyes and gnashing teeth. She made a cross with her fingers as though to ward the butcher off.

"Is she crazy?" the butcher asked Madge.

"She's a vegetarian," Madge answered, as though the butcher should have known better.

"Go away!" the baker screamed at the butcher. "Slaughterer!"

The butcher moved to retrieve her jacket, but as she neared the chair where her coat was hanging, the baker began to hurl abusive expletives her way with renewed fury.

"Would you mind leaving?" Madge gently begged the butcher. "I'll drive her home."

"Murderer! Butcher! You're a shameful member of the female gender!" screamed the baker, stamping her feet and shaking her fists.

An afternoon in Paradise quickly turned into a nightmare, and the butcher hurried out of the café. Mercifully there had been no other patrons in the place at the time, but her humiliation was devastating.

At home in her apartment, the baker's words of disgust rang loud in the butcher's ears. It was clear that the baker loathed the butcher's profession to such a degree that she rejected the butcher completely, even on a sexual level. It made no sense, but the butcher was madly in love, having been so definitely dismissed. She decided to lay low for awhile and avoid the bakery until the baker's desire obliterated her obvious prejudice.

The butcher began to buy her bread at a large grocery store around the corner from her shop. She rearranged her walking habits so that she never passed the bakery. She hoped that the baker would miss her, and also hoped that she could cure herself of her lovesickness. The butcher was a very strong-willed woman who, with a lot of sit-ups, could almost begin to forget her lust for the baker.

Sometimes her feelings would come rushing back. Little things reminded her of her love for the baker: putting away her cleaver at the end of the day, going home to an empty apartment, the sight of a bagel. These things made her weak for a moment, but she fought hard to forget.

One night, after a few glasses of beer with a friend, the butcher went home and stood in front of her full-length mirror. It was beyond her why the baker would reject her so fully. She looked into the mirror and considered the possible points against her but could find nothing dissatisfactory: her breasts, she thought, were rather nice. Big, but not daunting. Her legs were muscular but slender, the kind of legs that look good on vacation, shooting out of Bermuda shorts. Her belly was firm but not so toned as to be uninviting. Physically the butcher was a fine specimen of a woman, a perfect balance of sinew and softness; there was no threat of excessive sportiness in her physique. It had taken her thirty-seven years and a variety of seminars, but the butcher was rather fond of her body.

To hell with that baker, she decided, and went on with her life. Love was not everything. She was busy with her career, giving lectures on fine cuts of beef at the Women's Career Centre. She had her work and her sit-ups and her night-school. For three years she'd been studying gourmet vegetarian cooking. Had the baker bothered to take the time to see for herself, she would have realized what a well-rounded person the butcher was.

Everything was going nicely for the butcher in terms of her recovery from her lusty obsession with the baker. And then Madge ruined it all. She decided to have a party celebrating the cafe's ten-year anniversary. The butcher was invited. Because it was not every day that a women-only coffee shop celebrated a decade of business, the butcher felt obliged to go. She knew that the baker would be there, but decided to think of it as a test.

In preparing for the party, the butcher didn't think about the fact that the baker might not be there alone. And she wasn't.

When the butcher walked into the cafe, the first person she saw was the baker. She was no longer snarling and no longer had charming bits of baguette in her hair. She was with a woman. The woman was leaning all over the baker with her willowy body; she was tall and possessive and wore too many handpainted scarves. And she gave the butcher a hateful smile when the butcher stared at her. The butcher decided that if the woman was going to be that hostile, she might as well go ahead and get a really good look at the baker.

The baker smiled, ever-so-vaguely in the direction of the butcher, but she did not reveal her recognition. Madge stood nervously in the corner watching the whole scene. She was counting on the butcher's gentle ways, hoping things would remain civil. If the situation became unpleasant, she assumed that the butcher would leave graciously. But the butcher had no plans to leave. She was sick and tired of being the nice, complacent butcher.

"Oh, Jocasta, you're so funny!" The baker's laugh was the too-loud kind, the sort that reveals that its owner is having a rotten time. The willowy woman's name was Jocasta and she was busy charming the pants off everyone around her. It was hard for the butcher to watch them together and she slurped away at her beer, trying to guess how long they would last. Their happiness seemed false, temporary at best. Jocasta was clearly passionless, a hyper-mercurial sort who would soon tire of the baker's earthy sensuality. The butcher began to conduct an astrological analysis of them from across the room and then decided to approach the willowy one. She wanted to know one thing: what it was that Jocasta did for a living that made her so terrific in the eyes of the baker.

"Excuse me," the butcher began, almost gagging in the patchouli-mist that surrounded Jocasta.

The woman seemed to know exactly who the butcher was. She smiled benevolently down from her great height and said, "Yes?"

"What do you do for a living?"

The great and willowy Jocasta tossed her head back and laughed as if the question was the most delightful thing she had heard in a long time. The butcher wondered if she was an actress, the way Jocasta found everything so entertaining. With a flash of her ring-coated fingers she dug beneath her scarves and pulled out a card, which she handed to the butcher without a word. So insulted was the butcher by the woman's condescending air and dramatic sense of herself that she refused to read the card. She nodded at the baker and turned on her heel, leaving the café before her pride was damaged further.

But she could not resist looking at the card once she was out on the sidewalk. Her curiosity and rage were too great. On the Japanese paper, in swirls of silver ink, the butcher read:

Things of Beauty and Light by Jocasta
Candles and Crystals

She flicked the card into traffic and walked on, away from the café where the baker had stood looking more beautiful than ever. It was cruelty on the part of Fate that she should become more and more beautiful. And the butcher's dislike for Jocasta was based on more than jealousy. It was something unnameable that troubled the butcher's sensitive soul.

At about three a.m. her telephone rang. She had been dreaming about the baker and was disoriented. She fumbled with the receiver and finally answered, "Butcher speaking."

"It's Madge," said the quiet voice on the other end of the line.

"This is the butcher," the butcher said again, still half-asleep.

"Yes I know that," Madge said impatiently, "I need your help."

The butcher sat quickly upright in bed, imagining that something had happened to the café. "Go ahead, I'm here."

"We're at the jail-house," Madge whispered.

"We?"

"The baker and I, and Jocasta. I'm trying to get the baker to press charges but she won't."

The butcher rubbed her forehead in confusion, "I don't get it. Who's in jail?"

"Jocasta. Almost."

"What for, making pornographic candles?" The butcher was irritated.

"For assault," hissed Madge. "She hit the baker. And apparently it isn't the first time."

The butcher whistled through her teeth and said, "What do you want me to do?"

Madge sighed heavily and said, "Could you pick us up, say, in an hour? The baker keeps talking about you." The line was quiet and there was a shuffling sound. The butcher couldn't ask Madge what the baker was saying about her.

"Hi." It was the voice of the baker. The sound of her voice over a telephone wire made the butcher dizzy and she lay back on the bed to steady herself. "Can you come get us at the police station?"

"Do you love me?" asked the butcher, and then she wished she hadn't.

"No. Madge says you have a car. Could you pick us up?"

"Could you love me?" Again the butcher was direct.

"No. I have certain rules, certain beliefs. Can't you understand?"

"No, I can't. Let your beliefs call you a cab."

* * *

The butcher can love the baker but the baker can't love the butcher back, loving only the candlestick maker. Even if the candlestick maker hits her, she forgives her because she makes things of beauty and light. She is creative, and so redeems herself in the eyes of the baker. She creates instead of destroying. The baker can't say the same of the butcher. Everything the butcher stands for is about ugliness and suffering and violence. She might be beautiful to look at, but she is a murderer.

The baker refuses to leave Jocasta, no matter how often Madge urges her to. And the butcher still cares from a distance, though she's had to give up eating baked goods in an effort to control her feelings for the baker. She avoids all manner of buns and bread and especially bagels, and sticks to fruit and vegetables and tofu. She thinks about sending the baker a postcard telling her that she has been a vegetarian herself since 1978. But then there is the question of how the butcher can do what she does. How can she be a vegetarian *and* a butcher? To this day there are still many questions in the butcher's head. How can the baker care so much for animals and yet not for herself? The butcher comes from a long line of butchers on her mother's side. She wonders what the baker came from.

The Fishmonger's Wife

She had the sleek hardmuscled arms of a fishmonger's wife who never was. God how she touched things!: boys' skulls, melons in the market. And she roved her eyes. She tested things, assessed them. Roved them over flesh and fruit, calculating the sum and total worth of all she spent her eyes and touches on.

She was a calculator in workwoman's clothing.

I heard her clicking out costs: numbers fit like microscopic jigsaw pieces in her number-mad mind. She was divinely focused and so was oblivious to the fact that she was wanted by everyone she walked past. Her legs were hard wide gates that led to a delicious church, a pristine chapel where people prayed hard and begged for relief: hers and their own. She could have been, but never was, the fishmonger's wife.

She worked for the fishmonger, slicing up the smallest fish, weighing the paper-wrapped purchases that passed through her hands. Thus she spent the hours of her life, and that was penance enough.

He wanted her, but his want was not enough. His head swam with hopes of luring her into his kitchen where kettles steamed and women leaned hungry blades into swamps of scales and bellies. He wanted to promote her to a more murderous position so that he could watch her. But she was not ambitious and stayed near her counter up front, resisting him, his offers.

But her eyes roved, and he caught on that.

He begged her and said, "See what else I can show you! I can show you the ecstasies of lace and the *real* of life— the eggs and eyes picked from eyepocks with careful knifepoints. I can make you into an artist, show you these carcasses lovingly, as only a man to his wife. I'll waft your way not only Paris perfumes but the soothingest gales of gutrot."

She was steely when he murmured in his weakness, "Darling... the muscles in your arms..."

And then he went so far as to touch her, with the point of the knife he always carried. It was a careful touch, meant to convince her, but she fled.

She was not *his* to carve up a history with, not *his* to slash through the future with. He promised to be generous, but she knew in her dark heart that he wouldn't be, and so she ran, sacrificing coins and the joy of a job. Her insistent refusal offered her no safety from his ardent wishing.

With arms like that, with their striking ripples and cuts and cords of sinew twisting with every gesture, she ran, pausing only to test the infantile weight of a mandarin orange in her palm. She felt as light and continued to run. She could have been all kinds of things, but *wife* was not among them.

Obvious Need And Senseless Longing

I gave up drinking in favour of buying cookbooks. Whereas I had previously entertained only a passing interest in food, I soon came to worship it with the help of such picturesque manuals as the Joy Of and the Essentials Of. Which is not to say that I became a great cook, oh no. But I did evolve from a drunkard into a self-taught scholar of all things foodish. Money that once provided me with a week's worth of gin was better spent on a hardcover tome celebrating the history of canapes. Anyone willing to invest the time and money will soon see that the art of hors d'oeuvres is a great deal more complex than it seems from the outside. Sober, I realized that a great many things were far more complicated than I had drunkenly assumed. The act of eating, for example, is not simply the business of grab-and-chew. Despite their continual mention of wine accompaniment, cookbooks helped me to pry the perpetual bottle from my hands. No form of booze ever dazzled me in quite the same way once I discovered the world of descriptive cookery.

I've never stopped missing booze. It was my belief that to cease drinking was to cease longing. I never anticipated that booze would take up the gauzy role of *old flame* in my heart. Because I kicked it alone there was no pamphlet to warn me of its everlasting hold. After surviving the shakes and the cravings I was left with a sense of permanent nostalgia. I recalled thousands of wonderful nights of numbness, nights filled with great lovers and carefree comraderie. The erotic bounty I imagined existed when drunk disappeared with sobriety. I realized I wasn't terribly fond of most of the people in my life. But as I trudged celibately along my memory transformed my former life into a series of black-outs and bleary honeymoons. Everyone had looked so *good* then.

I needed an object of desire, a reason to stay sober. Martha Stewart provided me with just such inspiration. On rare occasions when Martha failed to stir me I turned to cooking shows and gourmet magazines until the fits of weakness subsided. My small London apartment was choked with stacks of cookbooks and magazines. In subscribing to clean living I subscribed to a great many magazines from all over the world. Every available surface was covered with glossy photo-packed descriptions of food-related topics: festivals, schools, kitchen design, etc. My liquor cabinet contained eleven different kinds of olive oil and my wine-rack was filled with various vinegars. Where some alcoholics replace booze with coffee and doughnuts, I substituted premium condiments.

My initial attachment to Martha Stewart was not sexual. It was completely innocent. She was my Betty Ford, my Betty Crocker. I didn't worry about my worship until I began to develop romantic feelings for her. Not that Martha isn't a fine-looking woman and worthy of lust. She'll always be a knock-out. But she wasn't really my type. For a time I accepted my desire for Martha. I framed the covers of her magazine and hung them over my bed. But when the faint erotic flicker became a libidinous obsession, I began to worry about myself. There was no self-help group that could help me if I lost control.

One afternoon I was hunched over my coffee table making a list of reasons why Martha and I would make a great couple. It was easy to come up with reasons why

Martha was a catch: She had a farmhouse in New England. She was blonde, rich and had her own magazine. She was probably too busy making crafty things to nag much. She wouldn't mind cooking most of the meals. The house would be tidy and seasonally decorated at all times... When the phone rang I was glad, because I was beginning to see a very unattractive side of myself.

"Hullo?"

"Darling, are you sitting down?" It was Gregory, my only friend in London.

"Yes, I'm sitting. What is it?"

"What? Have you got someone there or something?"

"No. Why do you ask?" I turned my list face-down on the table.

"You sound funny, like you're up to something."

"Gregory, you know damned well I haven't been up to anything since 1985!"

"Testy!"

"Look, if you have something to tell me then I wish you would *tell* it already. I'm busy falling in love with Martha Stewart over here."

Gregory gasped, "Are you drinking?"

"No, I am not drinking! Falling in love with home-making gurus is something sober people do."

"Mmmm. Well, listen. Someone died, love, and you're going to be very upset. But I can't come over to comfort you because I have an appointment."

"Who?"

"He's a film director, fortyish, nice car—"

"Who DIED, you idiot?" I was feeling unwell, antici-pating the bad news.

Gregory took a deep dramatic breath and whispered, "Elizabeth David." He paused and when I said nothing he tumbled out, "Oh darling, I'm *so* sorry. Will you be all right?"

I muttered that I would be fine and slammed down the receiver. I was not *fine*. No. I reeled with pain, the creeping kind that burns up the back of the throat. I set about clearing up the copies of Martha Stewart's *Living* magazine and my frivolous love-lists. No. The word pounded in my chest like a jackhammer. NO! NO! My guilt and sorrow were immense. How could I have been so unfaithful? The greatest food writer of all time had died while I was busy lusting after Martha Stewart. Elizabeth David lived and breathed food; Martha Stewart was just a symbol of American *zietgeist* and family values.

I will remember the pain of that afternoon for the rest of my life, the way the Kennedy assassination hangs in other people's hearts. Her poor family, I thought, going to the bookshelf where I proudly displayed my favourite foodbooks. I took down the well-thumbed copy of *An Omelette And A Glass Of Wine*. A tear slipped from my eye and I swatted it away. I clutched the book to my chest and wandered around the flat for hours. Finally I decided to go for a walk. I was determined to be fine.

On the way home I passed a wine shop. It had always been there, but I'd come to London after drying out and hadn't noticed it. I noticed it then and paused in front of the door. I tried old tricks: chanting my postal code, reminding myself of the upcoming nine-year anniversary of my sobriety. Nothing worked, and so I went into the shop and bought the most expensive Bordeaux they had. The man looked at me curiously, seeing the book still pressed to my chest and the tears in my eyes. He shrugged and handed me the bottle, neatly camouflaged in a paper sack that shouted HENRY'S FINE WINES! in red letters. I prayed that I wouldn't run into any of my neighbours on the way back to my flat.

Back upstairs again I set down the book and placed the bottle of wine in the centre of my dining room table. I contemplated it from all angles, pacing laps around it. I would sit down and have just one glass, a memorial toast. Pure terror kept me from opening the bottle though, and in my quandary I squeezed the corkscrew so fiercely that I cut my hand. It was one of my worst booze-dilemmas ever. I decided to leave the bottle on the table as a reminder of my weakness and went to bed, but not before turning every framed photo of Martha to face the wall. Beneath the sheets I said a prayer for Elizabeth David. And I wondered who had come up with the concept of the 12 Steps when it often felt more like the 39.

After several days of unrestrained mourning I felt much better. The bottle of wine sat on the table and I barely noticed it until Gregory called. He insisted that I meet him at nine o'clock the next morning. We were going to attend the Elizabeth David Estate Auction, he said. A friend of a friend had managed to secure our invitations. He gave me no opportunity to argue and hung up before I could protest.

In typical Gregory style, he failed to attend. Directions to the auction house were left on my answering machine at four a.m. in a rather sexually-satisfied voice. His work as a go-go caterer often led him to the beds of his clientele and it was no surprise to me that he cancelled. I decided that I would go anyway, even though I had my reservations about the ethics involved. It seemed sacrilegious to me that Ms. David's family would sell off her kitchen equipment. I wondered what kind of vicious family she had belonged to that they were cashing in on her measuring spoons and tattered recipe cards. As a kind of talisman I carried the bottle of wine in my handbag. Though unsure as to why I felt the need for it, I brought it along, counting on it to give me strength.

The auction was a miserable affair, cold and impersonal. People pretended grief as they eyed the displays of Ms. David's belongings. I purchased linen tea-towels and a chipped souffle cup. My money disappeared quickly as my sentimental side overtook my logic. Things were terribly over-priced; it was no cheap rummage sale. When a first-edition copy of *An Omelette And A Glass Of Wine* went up on the block I stifled a cry. The opening bid was higher than my bank balance, never mind what I carried in my wallet.

An exceptionally good-looking young woman captured the prize. She remained outwardly calm but I could sense her excitement as she marched forward to sign for her purchase. She clutched it to her breasts and smiled brilliantly at me as she passed by. Before good sense could deter me I followed her to the exit and fell into step behind her on the street. She seemed to take no notice of me and I pursued her wonderfully swaggering hips for several blocks before she turned around.

"Are you following me?" she asked, laughing coyly. She had a New York accent and bright red lipstick. She still clutched the book protectively.

I scrambled for an explanation and then blurted out, "I just wanted to congratulate you." With these words I took the bottle of wine from my bag and thrust it at her, offering no further information.

She accepted the wine and stood staring at me with her dark eyes, as though waiting for me to say something more. The way she chewed her lip made me feel quite dizzy and adolescent.

"I bought it but I decided that I should give it to someone who needs it less than I do," I said. She was staring across the street at the Thames and I wasn't sure if she heard me. The bottle hung loosely in one of her hands, threatening to crash to the pavestones.

Finally she said, "Well, thank-you, but I don't drink. *Can't* actually." She handed me the bottle and then smiled brightly, "What did you get at the auction?"

"A few gadgets. Spent every pound I had with me."

"Why did you buy the wine?" she asked softly.

"I was having a moment of doubt."

"Would you like to walk for a bit?"

I nodded and we strolled along. She explained to me how much she missed wine. The taste of it, the way it enhanced food and conversation. How she even missed the hangovers.

"Really? I don't know if I miss hangovers," I said, shaking my head. "All that aspirin, all those lost mornings..."

She stopped and looked at me, then moved in close. I could smell shampoo and stale cigarettes as she took my arm, "I miss having a reason for feeling bad."

For a few blocks we didn't talk much. Maybe I did miss having an excuse for bad days. But this was a good day, a grand one. I felt drunk walking beside her and began to wonder what possible misery had ever plagued me.

"Shall we go on?" I asked, suddenly aware that we had marched into a residential area. When she looked at me nervously I added, "I mean, is an omelette just as good without a glass of wine?"

"I hate omelettes," she giggled. "It's the glass of wine I miss."

It turned out we were standing in front of the building where her flat was. When she invited me in for lunch I couldn't think of a good reason not to accept. The old devil of lust was rising up in me and it felt marvelous.

"Are you sure you know how to cook?" I teased, setting

the bottle of wine down on the stone steps outside her place.

While she prepared lunch I asked her why someone so young would feel the need to quit drinking. She was only twenty-nine. I assumed everyone was as slow to learn as I was.

"I had to start taking care of myself," she said. "I was drinking an awful lot."

"How much is a lot, anyway? I've always wondered, even since I stopped drinking, what other people considered to be *a lot*. Is it a drink every day? A bottle of gin every night? Getting soused every weekend?"

She smiled, "I guess when *a lot* turns into *too much*, you need to stop."

"But what's too much?" I insisted. Lunch was smelling awfully good. *Too good*. I told her so.

"You're stubborn, aren't you? Won't take things simply, huh? You still miss drinking."

"All the time," I said. "It makes no sense sometimes, how much I miss it. I pine for it. But I've learned to live without it I guess."

While we ate I showed her the items I purchased at the auction. With great amusement she held up the chipped souffle cup and raised an eyebrow.

"Obvious need," I assured her, and leaned over the rubble of our devoured meal to taste her red mouth.

When I left her building much later that evening I noticed that the bottle of Bordeaux had been snapped up by some unseen wine-lover. I looked up at the window of her flat and suddenly understood the pleasure of longing. It wasn't always without sense nor completely separate from need.

In The Spice House

When I first met you I didn't know a bay leaf from a Maple Leaf. The idea of tossing leaves into a perfectly good sauce frightened me. But you were so confident, holding your head high as you marched me to the Spice House in Kensington and took me down the aisle where the bay leaves lived. We visited six countries with our nostrils: you put your smooth-warm hand on my arm by the tins of hearts of palm. There had been no kiss between us, not then, but you pointed to the packets of saffron and I was all over you with my mouth.

That afternoon you took me to your little apartment. We usually met for very public coffees and lunches, platonic interludes in crowded spaces. Movie theatres, libraries and darkened bars were unconsciously avoided. But as you set the grocery bags down to struggle with the uncooperative lock on your door I was oblivious to our sudden *aloneness*. Instead I studied your perfectly rolled shirtsleeves and the back of your very fine head. I lost myself in a reverie of trying to guess your hat size, trying to imagine the way your skull tilted when you were listening intently. Oh you: beautiful.

I stepped into your apartment with hungry eyes and a greedy stomach. The sunsplashed hallway, the numerous healthy plants, the window at the end of the hall: I took them all in, eye-gulping the details. You took my hand and led me past a small room with no door: your *reading room*. A shrine of books, but not nearly as important as your kitchen. I knew that you would take me to the kitchen first.

"It's a really small place," you warned me on the street-car, as though I would mind.

We stood in the doorway and looked in at the kitchen. I saw a fairly large room, well-equipped, with shelf after shelf of mason jars, full of powders and spices that were clearly labelled by your neat hand. White refrigerator, red stove, a ceiling fan spinning above our heads as we moved into the room. A light perfume of foods previously cooked tangoed with the mingling perfumes of herbs hanging to dry.

"Sit down," you said, and pointed to a small bed in one corner of the room. There was no kitchen table, there were no chairs.

"Your bed is in the kitchen?" I asked. I worried that you were odd, that you had other strange habits I hadn't detected. Perhaps your passionate niceness was a smoke-screen for strangeness.

"It's a small apartment. I told you," you said, turning to the shelves and touching various jars.

I went to the corner and sat on the edge of the bed. My deep desire for you didn't guarantee an absence of fear. My hands were damp as I watched you bustling with the groceries. I didn't want my nervousness to threaten the development of our romance.

"A friend of mine in New York has a bathtub in her living room," I offered.

You nodded in acknowledgement and continued tossing cut vegetables into a large pot. There was a moment's pause as you made stern-faced selections from your spice-collection. Royal choices: you held each jar of spice like each was a precious trophy or an urn of sacred ashes.

Soon a gorgeous smell began to leak out of the pot and into the room. You sauteed shrimp and talked to me, grinning happily and winking. The smells combined and grew more intense as we talked. My hunger was becoming a drunkeness, teased by the wild aromas of your lunch-making.

"The stew has to simmer for quite awhile," you said, sitting next to me.

"What kind of stew is it?" I asked.

"It's an Indian vegetable stew, but I like to add shrimp. I hope you like it. But it has to cook really slowly and for a long time. Do you mind?"

I *did* mind because the smell was intoxicating and unbearable. The room was full of the warmth and the tingling tickle of the meal; and there was my ache for you. The two longings inseparable, my hunger was confused in its priorities. My head swam with the perfumes of your culinary seductiveness.

That first afternoon in your apartment: the wild exquisite smell of your skin and of spices. We rocked together on the bed while the stew grew thicker and hotter; we simmered like the pot on the stove: ground and stirred weeks of built-up wanting.

You sat up and announced, "Lunchtime." It was nine o'clock at night. The sky had blackened outside the window. You stood naked at the stove and stirred your potion, an unforgettable sight in shadows.

Naked, we ate the stew in bed, a divine meal with your thigh resting against mine. We said nothing: there was the scraping of our spoons and the traffic outside, the fridge purring. I discovered that the kitchen was the perfect place for a bed. Stomachs full and heads full of fading spices, we slept on the bed in the corner of your kitchen, soundly and all night.

In the Spice House

Before you I never cared what went into my mouth in the way of nourishment. My appetite was scarce, dispassionate. Love, too, was sporadic and thoughtless, and I had certainly never tasted authentic passion.

You always insisted that I meet you at the Spice House. Often I arrived there early, to drive myself crazy with anticipation. I'd lurk behind stacks of Ethiopian bread, behind veils of sweet-grass: to watch your entrance. Once, in a playful mood, you brought me to the edge of a ribald moan in a shadowy corner of the shop, next to a giant drum of curry powder that burnt my throat and nostrils as I gasped in pleasure. Your hand could always stir me just so.

We met like that on Saturdays: in the Spice House and then on to your house. You'd put something torturously good-smelling on to simmer or in to bake, like some people put soft music on, and we would end up eating lunch at midnight, propped up by pillows.

You gave me your Saturday, your Sunday morning. Questions were distasteful to you and you swatted them away like flies. Of me you wanted to know everything, but you insisted you could not offer the same revelations. In my blind contentment I agreed to your conditions.

* * *

One Saturday you didn't show up at the Spice House. I waited until the shopkeeper asked me to leave. You weren't a *telephone person*; wouldn't have one, wouldn't use one. I went home and wondered if I had the right to drop by your house. I wandered around my own kitchen, its cupboards filled with the little bags of spice you sent me home with every Sunday morning. Neatly labelled, carefully tied.

"Someday we'll get you some nice jars for your spices," you said. You never came to *my* apartment.

Unable to eat but absolutely starved, I took the bus to your little apartment.

Your lock was cheap. You didn't answer my knocking, my soft calls. I remember thinking it was far too easy to get in. The doorknob was in my hands in pieces after a few frantic wrenchings. The smell of burning food was strong and I ran down the hallway to your kitchen, blinded by the black smoke that filled the apartment and stung my eyes.

I stood in the doorway. Hanging there, you said nothing, offered no explanation.

I turned off the burner, sat on the bed in the corner of your kitchen and looked up at you. There was a wooden chair on its side on the floor. A chair I had never been offered and had never seen in any other room.

* * *

Your father gave me the urn with your ashes inside.

"I guess you're the girlfriend," he shrugged. He drove off, back to a distant city I hadn't known you were from.

I went back to your little apartment with the urn and put a key in the new lock. Your mother asked me to deal with your belongings, your things. Your nice jars, the white refrigerator and red stove. Strange to suddenly have a key, to have access to your secrets. But I decided I would not read anything, wouldn't look in drawers, wouldn't scan the spines of your books with curious eyes.

The big pot you liked best I filled with water.

One by one I pulled jars from shelves and dumped their contents into the water as it boiled. Incompatible spices were mixed together. I threw them all in. I cried as I dumped and scooped your ashes into the pot. The smell was heady, rancid and peppery. I lay down on the bed and took a deep breath, missing you and feeling hungry; the confused appetite I had always enjoyed in your little apartment.

When the soup had cooked down to a thick, grainy sludge I turned off the heat. All those weeks I had been so cold, unable to warm myself in any way. I undressed in your kitchen, shivering near the red stove. I carried the pot of acrid soup to the side of the bed and sat down. Ladling the warm mixture onto my belly, I smeared myself with the pasty soup of spices and you. I massaged it into my breasts and thighs, remembering our Saturday afternoons, every one.

Completely covered, mummified in the warm paste, I stretched out flat on the sheets and studied the chair you never offered me. It sat upright by the white fridge. I realized as I made myself warmer with eager muck-covered fingers that I had known you almost longer in your death than I had in life.

The next morning I dressed without washing, pulled my clothes over the crust on my skin. I took the urn to my apartment. I filled it with one of the bags of spice you had given me. I have a nice jar now and six chairs to offer no one.

Tantrum

They say she's been fired from three big restaurants. Still, someone will always hire her. She's good at what she does. The firings are mysterious, the reasons unknown. No one knows the truth, they just make it up as she goes along. Her underlings watch her from a safe distance, whispering and speculating behind their hands.

Somehow, despite her soft-spoken ways and the gentle sway of her long body, she has earned the nickname Tantrum. She goes by the name herself, enjoying the joke. There is a good natured-wickedness there, something half-hungry in her grin. It's nice working under her, pleasant to take her orders and follow them. She comes in cheery, heads home laughing. There is no obvious danger in her demeanor. She teases us; is easy to work for. Easy to think about all night long without meaning to.

I'm happily married, easily distracted.

The kitchen is winding down for the afternoon. Tantrum waves me over to her work station, holding up a bottle of cold white wine. There are a few others bustling around the kitchen, performing their last-minute clean-up duties. I lean against the chilly stainless steel of her work table and accept a glass of wine. My father always told me to drink with the Boss; for once I like my father's words.

Tantrum takes up a lime and slits it wide open, palming the halves. She points to the pale green pulp and smiles. She tells me that my eyes are exactly the same colour as a perfect lime. We drink another glass of wine and she insists on calling me Margarita. Tells me how she loves limes and angry sous chefs. Before I can tell her that I'm seldom angry, she re-corks the wine and puts on her coat, bidding me farewell.

I hate the way she makes me feel: lust-mad and empty, all at once.

"This is a shiitake, *this* is a portabello," she scolds. The young apprentice standing next to her nods meekly. I'm consumed with jealousy and turn away. All day I have been watching her, peering at her around braids of garlic, stalking her through steam-clouds. I try to tell myself how ridiculous it is, this *desire*. I am faithful. I am always *fidele*.

"You're talking to yourself again," she teases, standing just behind me.

"It improves the roux," I say, sounding edgy.

Tantrum takes the spoon away from me and tastes for herself. She doesn't bother to test the temperature, she simply plunges the hot spoonful into her mouth. I feel as though I have ingested something too hot: my belly boils and sweats.

"Tell the roux I say hello," she murmurs, walking away from me. Her apron is low-slung around her hips, her hands swing loose. The white of her chef's jersey is blinding, the sleeves rolled high against her hard, brown arms. It takes so little to captivate me now: the merest bounce of her damp pony-tail, the coil of it grazing her shoulder-blades. Any movement or word. I stir the roux unnecesarily and glare at her back. I begin to hope that they end up firing her, for any reason at all.

"Are you angry with me?" Tantrum asks this after I have tried to avoid looking at her for a full week.

"No, of course not," I reply.

"Do you have a very bad temper?" she asks softly, trying to catch my gaze.

"I have a long fuse but a vicious temper," I warn. I'm only half-joking with her. The closer she moves, the more agitated I become. Although I'm generally quite serene, she brings out an irritable side of me I don't quite understand.

"Would you ever throw a tantrum for me, here in the kitchen?" She wears a chiding grin. "In front of everyone?"

I shake my head very definitely NO.

"Privately then?"

Shock and surprise overwhelm me. She fixes her gaze upon me relentlessly. I throw a towel at her and blush. Throwing something at her excites me; I've no idea why. She picks up the towel and wraps it around her hand, continues to stare without blinking.

And then I hear myself inviting her out for dinner. It seems ludicrous, the boldness in my voice. I don't ask people to go anywhere, ever. She is nodding yes the whole time I am wondering how to withdraw my invitation. In a whirl of seconds she decides that tonight would be best. After work suits her fine.

"Where should we go?" she asks. "I hate most restaurants."

"You decide then," I say, my mouth dry.

Tantrum glances at her watch and then looks around the kitchen. Her voice drops lower and she says, "My place. Two conditions though. You can come over, but you can't come into my kitchen and you can't tell anyone here that we met outside work. Deal?"

All afternoon I try to imagine calling my husband to tell him I have dinner plans. Sounding natural is an impossibility. I opt for not calling at all and watch Tantrum from across the kitchen. She is showing a group of school children on a tour how to chop vegetables safely and swiftly. Her knife rocks skillfully through several stalks of celery, the blade flying. I watch her fingers balanced on the knife-handle, the murderous look of calm on her face. The children are in awe and so am I.

"How's the margarita, Margarita?" she calls from her sacred kitchen. I am lounging on her sofa, pretending to like Eric Satie. In my attempt at seeming calm I am getting very drunk.

"Wonderful," I call back.

There is a great deal of banging going on in the kitchen. Exquisite smells waft forth, but the noise is horrific. She never slams things around this much at work.

I ask her if she needs any help and she emerges from the kitchen with a fresh drink for each of us. She sits with her thigh jammed up against mine on the small sofa and tosses most of the new margarita down her throat in one gulp. She seems completely sober, disconcertingly so. She slaps my leg and jumps back up, returning to the kitchen in easy strides. I sit staring at the spot that stings on my leg.

It becomes clear that any conversation we have will be conducted at screaming volume, what with the nervous piano music tumbling from the speakers and the blood thundering in my head.

"Where else have you worked?" I screech.

"All over."

"Which restaurant's been your favourite so far?"

"I don't have a favourite."

I feel incredibly irritated by her evasive answers. Shouting over the music, the tequila, the throbbing itch between my thighs: all of it makes me very angry. I snap off the stereo and feel relieved of at least some of the annoyance. I've never found wanting someone so infuriating before.

"Don't like Satie, do you?" she asks after a moment's pause. Again there is a great deal of banging and scraping coming from the kitchen. I take several long swallows of my drink to ease the scratching in my throat so that I can answer her.

"Just not in the mood for him—" there is a smashing of glasses that cuts me off and I reflexively rush into the kitchen to see if she is all right.

"Get the fuck out of here!" she snarls at me, standing in a pile of smashed glassware. I am taken aback by her sudden ferocity. My eyes fall upon the wall behind her. The entire wall is fitted with racks, racks holding hundreds of knives. It's quite terrifying to see so many all in one place, displayed like that. They're admirable as a collection, but Tantrum doesn't appear to like my admiration.

"OUT!" she screams at me. When I fail to move she grabs me roughly by the collar and drags me out of her kitchen. Her clawlike grip is hot through my shirt. I try to wriggle out of her clutch but am clumsy from the booze. I can't even look at her face because of the way she is holding me and pushing.

"Okay!" I shout. "I won't come into your goddamn kitchen! Jesus!" It's been a very long time since I've bellowed at someone. But her grip instantly releases, and when I turn to face her she is smiling brilliantly at me and giggling. To my great surprise I feel even more aroused by her mean laughter. Something in the kitchen is burning. She points to the sofa, indicating that I will sit back down, and goes back into the kitchen to check on the food.

Although I'm quite drunk, I want another drink. And I want another glimpse of that knife collection. Surely she won't mind if I ask for a refill, I think, moving to the kitchen doorway. In my effort to be quiet I manage to scrape my rings against the door-frame and she whirls around. This time she is completely enraged by my presence in her kitchen. Her reaction transcends mere anger. Reaching up she grabs one of the largest carving knives I have ever seen from a rack over the stove. Light glints off the blade of it and her free hand flies up into my face with a wicked slap. I fall to the floor. In a haze of surprise and my own fury I rise up and lean far forward into her face. Boozy hot breath escapes from between her red lips. I know she is holding the knife somewhere near my stomach, the cool of the blade brushes past my hand.

"You wouldn't," I whisper.

"My kitchen," she shrugs.

"It's nice," I parry. Her knuckle digs into my hip bone.

"I asked you to stay out of here."

"And what if I refuse?" I sneer.

She laughs, bitterly. "You're such a bored little housewife, aren't you? I can tell. I've seen you fantasizing. Ever heard the old saying, 'Careful what you wish for'?"

I feel my face grow hot. She lets out a bitchy laugh. I'm tempted to spit in her face, if only to relieve my humiliation. Have I been so obvious in my desire?

Her eyes go suddenly flat, then devoid of any fire. "You'd better go home," she says, pushing me away from her. She throws the knife into the sink and keeps her back to me.

"I'm not leaving until I've eaten," I say, folding my arms defiantly across my chest. Tantrum looks at me with such disgust that I wonder if she really means it. That I should leave. I don't want to. Our mouths were so close, our stomachs separated by a knife-blade. I've come too far to stop now. I tell her so.

"Too *far?*" Her eyes are flickering slightly.

"Yeah. I'm not leaving. Tell me, why is it that you've been fired so many times? Everyone at work is dying to know..."

The key is turned again, the lock on her temper picked with a question. Her eyes ignite with rage and she turns to her racks, grabbing for a knife. Then she flies at me, cat-crazy, hissing, swearing, lunging. I back away from her, not taking my eyes off her until I am forced to run into the living room to avoid batlike swipes of the knife she carries. In my flight I smash my leg on her glass coffee-table. A river of blood gushes from my shin and Tantrum sees it and howls with laughter. Again she lunges at me with the knife.

"Enough!" I scream, hopping away from her.

"I've come too far now," she mimics. Her sing-song voice sends a chill through me. Her voice sounds unreal, and so unlike her usual gravelly murmur. I hold up a hand to stop her and she swings the knife at it. I wonder if she has killed people; if the mystery surrounding her is much darker than I realized.

"C'mon darlin'," she coos. She grabs a handful of my shirt and twists the cloth tight until it pinches my skin. I try to slap her away but can't connect because of the angle she holds me at. "I don't think you know what *too far* really means. Did you want to go to bed with me? Is that what you thought you'd like, to get in my bed?" Her voice is a growl, a distillery breeze blowing hot pure alcohol and spit. "Or did you just want a little *kiss* so you could say you're open-minded?"

God forgive me, but I still want to get into bed with her. I scare myself. I nod yes to the wrong question.

She shoves me toward a door and orders me to open it. She holds the butt of the knife at the base of my spine and I fumble with the doorknob. The room behind this door is black. We step into it, into the coolness and quiet. I hear the door shut behind me. She no longer holds onto my clothes. She simply stands behind me, breathing up and down my vertebrae. I can feel her smile on the back of my skull.

I am standing with my bloody shin nudged up against something hard. Her bed? Tantrum lifts my shirt up and over my head and whistles through her teeth. With one of her hot hands she pushes me forward and I tumble clumsily, my knees cracking down on an unforgiving surface. I feel a thin sheet as I stretch my palms out in front of me. She is caressing me and pushing me, dragging her knuckles down my spine. I'm wet, terrified and confused: this can't be her bed...

"On your back," she hisses. There is a shudder of venetian blinds over my head. Slivers of light spill across me and a knife-blade gleams in the darkness. I hear the sound of her zipper, see the white flash of her shirt coming off. Sounds and sights are disconnected for me as I lay on my back, forcing myself to breathe. She yanks on the cord leading to the blinds again, letting in more light so that I can see her.

Tantrum is naked now except for an apron hung low around her waist. She is holding a carving knife and raises it above her head with both hands wrapped around the handle. My eyes snap shut as the wind of the blade rushes past my cheek. The blade is firmly planted in the wood next to my shoulder. I have decided that nothing but wood could make for such a hard mattress. She yanks on the knife and pulls it free. She straddles me, again raises the knife, again lets it fall within inches of my body. Near my leg. Alongside my neck. It swoops and thuds, and I don't scream, and wherever she chooses to bring the blade down is where an explosion of delighted terror rips through my skin.

I emit a mixed cry of pleasure-terror when she brings it down hard in the space between my parted knees. She brings it down closer and closer. I'm on the edge of horrified ecstasy. She leans over me and kisses me, seeking my mouth out with her blazing tongue and gnashing teeth. I hear the knife swooping down one last time and feel the shudder of the bed as she brings it down hard above my head. And she leaves it there, and takes me, the knife always within reach.

There is sunlight searing my eyelids when I wake. My head throbs ever so lightly, and it is when I roll over on my side that I remember where I have spent the night. The bed under me is hard, unforgiving: yet I have slept so well. Sitting up, I look around at the walls. Row upon row and rack upon rack of knives cover the walls. The sun sparkles on various blades. This collection is arranged according to size. I see the deep gouges in the wooden platform under me where Tantrum brought her chosen knife down. I sit on a giant chopping block, not a bed at all, the sun streaming cheerfully across the walls of knives.

There is no one else in the house as I pad naked from room to room. I obediently avoid the kitchen and see a note on the coffee table next to a glass of orange juice. Tantrum is nowhere to be seen.

You've called in sick. Remember
Condition Number Two?
Tantrum

I sip the juice and contemplate calling home to my husband, who by this time must be either furious or heartsick. It seems too difficult to tackle just then, and I return to Tantrum's bedroom. Stretched out on her mysterious bed

I think about everything I've known in the world and the things I haven't known.

Tantrum will probably disappear again and I'm almost glad. I'm delighted to learn that a potential for extremes exists. I like knowing that my pendulum can swing from comfort to terrorized joy. I just hope I haven't come too far to go back. There's the small matter of my husband... he doesn't care for knives.

One Lip

My wife tells me she is bored with me now, deeply bored. That I haven't *evolved* as a person at all. In desperation I cut off my lower lip with the biggest bread knife we own. *Now* I am different. Now she'll love me, I think to myself. She'll have no excuse for boredom! But I am wrong. She *hates* me without a bottom lip.

I tell her it will be like kissing a completely different person. She shakes her head, packs her suitcases and puts them in *my* station wagon.

"Hey," I ask, "which one of us is leaving?"

"Whose car is it?" she bellows.

"Mine," I answer slowly, because slowly is how I have to speak with only one lip. "You can keep the car if you don't leave me," I plead, mopping at my bloody chin with a rag.

She doesn't answer; she simply gnashes her teeth and looks out at the driveway. She's always hated my bottom lip, my taste in cars.

"Love you," I whimper. Hard to say, that one, with one lip, and still sound meaningful.

"You look *ridiculous*," she snarls. "What in the hell is wrong with you, anyway? Is *this* what I've married?" She grabs the bloodied rag and waves it in my face. I have to admit that the sight of my own mouthblood makes me dizzy and disgusted.

My wife starts to cry. I'd thought it would impress her, the lip thing, as an act of devotion. A new and passionately different me. It *does* make a big difference in my appearance. It's a *kind* of personal evolution.

"Kiss me," I say, taking her hands in mine.

"Ugghh," she moans, making a nasty face and wriggling away.

"WHAT MORE DO YOU WANT?" I scream. I feel like I'll do just about anything to keep her from leaving me.

"I want you to have two lips," she says flatly.

"Oh. I see."

She sighs. "You've changed the *wrong* way is all."

"Were you planning to leave me before I did this?" I ask, pointing to my one-lipped mouth.

"No!" she says. And I am horrified. But I can see that she is lying because she is knotting the hem of her blouse the way she always does when she is lying.

"Liar! You told me you were bored before I did this. Suitcases always follow declarations of boredom!" The harder I cry, the more blood squirts onto my clean white shirt. I hope she'll stay long enough to wash it. She knows about stains, the science of them.

"Okay. It's true. I've been planning to leave you for a long time," she admits.

"*How* long?" I demand. I need the details, and a Kleenex.

"Awhile now. I've been bored for a long time. I'm sorry." She knots and knots her blouse like the liar that she is.

"Kiss me," I say, moving into her and grabbing her blouse-knots in my fists. When I kiss her she makes a gagging sound and then suddenly, she lets go and kisses me back. Her mouth falls into mine and a warm liquid spills between us. She kisses me with more passion than she's shown in eight years. As we kiss I realize I have always hated the way she smells. The smell of her skin has always been a sexual obstacle. I pull away.

"Listen. I'll be honest too," I say. "I hate the way you smell. You smell like old bread. Like rotting dough or something. I'm sorry."

I realize then that I don't mind if she leaves me. I hope, in fact, that she will. The bread smell is rising in the room. I don't even mind if she takes the station wagon after all. She can take the damned car and fill it full of her dough-stink. I realize it all clearly now: I don't even love her. Have I ever? The pain in my mouth is making me rather philo-sophical.

"Well," she smiles meanly, "if you hate the way I smell so much, maybe you should have cut off your nose instead." And I know that she plans to stay. She has decid-ed to stay, it's clear. Now that she knows I *want* her to leave, she'll stay and stay.

While I wait patiently for her to get fed up with me and leave, the place where my lip used to be heals over into a lovely hard ridge of a scar. People are fascinated with it. Other women want to kiss me. I let them. My wife still complains that I am limited and shallow, but not as often. She knows that a lot of people are interested in me, and so she hangs on. I don't know if other people are kissing my wife, and I don't much care. Perhaps she has evolved beyond kissing. Most of the time she doesn't say a word.

To Market, To Market

To market, to market, to buy a fat pig,
Home again, home again, jiggety-jig.

I

The Lady Cab Driver, red-maned and temperamental, her glove-compartment full of loose Tarot cards and cigarettes, pulls her shiny yellow Checker cab down the boulevard. She looks to her left and to her right, smelling the perfume of her own curls as she turns each way. Across the intersection a man waves to get her attention. She guns the motor and roars through the intersection faster than is necessary. The thought of a silvery glass of gin for breakfast makes her impatient and reckless.

She always has a tall glass of straight-up Tanqueray before crashing to sleep in the morning. While the rest of the world is busy with its jack-hammers, squealing its brakes and craning its cranes, she expects herself to sleep. She drives all night and sleeps all day, a vampirical way of living that is at odds with almost everything jovial and lively. The gin comes in handy as a numbing agent and odour-killer: the house where she rents a room is filled with the smell of frying eggs twenty-four hours a day. The stench intensifies between the morning hours of eight and ten, just as she is curling up to sleep. Morning and all of its smells becomes more and more unbearable as she gets older.

In the afternoon she lights a cigarette and hides under a crocheted blanket, peers out one of the many holes in the yarn, smokes through one woolen port-hole and watches TV through another. Under the afghan she is safe from sunlight and the stale stink of frying that clouds the house where she rents a room.

Recalling the details of her daily routine makes her feel a bit sick to her stomach. The man who waved to her on the corner is climbing into the back seat of the cab while the Lady Cab Driver is still lost in her reverie. As the smell of rye whiskey and Blue Stratos fills the cab she returns to the sharpness of reality. Anxious to smoke, the man offers her a cigarette. She declines and waits for his instructions. He seems too friendly, a category she subdivides into friendly-as-in-drunk or friendly-as-in-psychotic. She leans toward the latter.

His cologne makes her head ache and she rolls her window down an inch, marveling at the unseasonably cold night air as it blasts across her cheek.

"I'm going over to my girlfriend's place," he says, exhaling loudly.

"Does she live on any particular street or should I drive up and down them all?" The Lady Cab Driver is surprised at her own sourness. She feels more agitated than usual.

He tells her the address and laughs softly as they move into traffic, "She's not *really* my girlfriend. I'd like her to be."

"Unrequited love is difficult," she nods, trying to sound a little more pleasant. It wasn't good to provoke them.

"I want her to meet me and see how good-looking I am."

The Lady Cab Driver feels the stone of her heart roll over cold in its chamber.

"You haven't *met* her yet?"

"Nuh. I've been waiting to."

"You *do* realize that it's three in the morning?"

"That's when she gets home. She's a nurse. She eats Mexican food with another nurse and then she goes home. She's got white-blonde hair and little fat hips." He is silent for a moment and then sings out, "She moves like a little piglet! To market, to market!"

The childlike quality of his giggle makes the Lady Cab Driver want to throw up on the dashboard. For a few blocks she just drives. She doesn't want to drop this guy off at a house where he isn't expected. It is obvious that the woman has no idea who he is, but that he knows too much about her. He sits looking serenely out the cab window as they cruise along and the Lady Cab Driver wonders what the least conspicuous route to the Muldana Hospital would be.

"Or... I could catch her and put her in a bottle. So I can watch her!" he says suddenly. Every time he speaks it startles the Lady Cab Driver like a surprise gun shot. She hears an oceanic roaring in her ears and touches down hard on the brakes. She sits for a few seconds, trying to clear the pounding from her head so that she can speak.

"I think I'm going to let you out here," she says firmly. She tries to focus on the glare of the 7-11 sign further down the boulevard. She wishes she had stopped somewhere more public and curses her own foolishness. The area around them is isolated but for the convenience store. It's a dead stretch between more populated neighbourhoods.

"You're a shitty driver," he says.

"Consider it a free ride three quarters of the way, okay? I'm not taking you any further tonight."

"We're so close, I can be there in two minutes on foot. You think you're doing someone a big favour don't you? Let me tell you that you're only making things worse."

She decides to radio for the cops as soon as he gets out of the car. He opens his door slowly and swings his legs out, remaining seated. She can feel his eyes on the back of her head.

"I'm only *kidding around* for God's sake!" he shouts, laughing. "I'm going to my sister's place. Jesus, maybe you should get into another line of work if you're this nervous..."

In the rearview mirror she can see him sweating and grinning, a grin that involves the exposure of his top two teeth.

"I'm an *actor!* I'm gonna' be in a play downtown. I play a guy who's a bit crazy. I was just rehearsing, practicing my *craft*."

"Rehearse somewhere else, asshole, you're not funny."

He sighs and shakes his head. "Well, that just shows me a little something. That some of us should accept our limitations in this world. Maybe go back to needlepoint and leave the car in the garage after eight o'clock at night!"

With that he slams out of the cab, taking his cloud of cologne and rye with him. He saunters away from the car slowly, heading for the 7-11 sign. She shakes her head to stop the ringing and roaring. It happens more often than she is comfortable with, the strange aural manifestation of her rage and fear. He taunted her about making things worse. She watches him stroll down a street where she would have to run. What would be traumatic for her, being left on the side of the road in the wee hours, is just the beginning of his adventure. He *swaggers*, is calm. The Lady Cab Driver thinks of the woman with the white-blonde hair coming home from work. Maybe she unlocks the door without fear; or maybe she looks around nervously, praying for a certain kind of sameness and uneventfulness. Visitors are probably not part of her plan for the night. Maybe she's looking forward to kicking her shoes into the corner and pouring herself a silvery glass of gin...

He just *flew*.

For such a big strapping fellow, he flew along like a feather before slapping down on the asphalt. When the yellow Checker took the first bite out of his strut, when he flew upward, she couldn't hear the sound of him splitting across the hood over the radio. She had turned it up loud. The brakes slammed hard and she backed the cab up, then screamed forward again as he tried to raise himself up from the pavement. His face disappeared in the white fog of the headlights.

She got out to look. He was still, with one sock-foot twitching and twisted in the wrong direction. She located his shoe a few feet away and put it in the glove-compartment. There was a great deal of blood on the road, but no cars came from either direction. With difficulty she dragged him into the back seat of the taxi. Her thin arms strained but she was surprised and delighted by her own unexpected strength. She closed the back door and looked in at him. She had his body; she had both of his shoes.

The Lady Cab Driver headed for the north-bound exit out of the city. Her glass of gin would have to wait. While she drove she scooped the contents of the glove-compartment into her purse, including the bloodied shoe. She watched the spattered body in the back seat rock as she changed lanes. She reached back behind herself and pushed him over. In struggling to do so she nearly missed the off-ramp she was looking for. At the last possible safe moment she veered onto the shoulder of the road at the mouth of the ramp.

It was still dark and cold when she walked away from her cab. She left it there on the side of the road, hazard lights flashing. It was a complicated climb out of the expressway system. Unaware of the hour, except that morning had not yet begun to light the sky, she walked quickly with the image of the white-blonde woman in her head. All she wanted was for the woman to be curled up safely in bed, no longer forced to suffer comparisons to piglets on their way to slaughter.

The walk downtown was all boulevards and long blocks. At seven thirty she reached the edge of the meat-packing district. Big trucks rumbled past her, shaking their crates of cargo. There was a faint smell of sawdust and blood on the wind. Her legs ached and her throat burned from Winstons and exhaust fumes and thirst. She would have been sipping her gin by then, she thought to herself. Rage had spoiled ritual and her good deed had made it necessary for her to run. She was heading for the lakeshore, far from her rented room and her bottle of Tanq. She could have been sipping gin through a hole in her blanket, oblivious to little fat hips and the frying of eggs.

There was an industrial section of the market where trucks re-fueled and lined up for repairs. The loading docks were full of fork-lifts and dollies and people shouting instructions. She kept moving until she reached the public section of the market, a pedestrian zone marked off by a gate. It had been a long time since she had stood at that gate. It was a threshhold offering a kind of old freedom. Stepping into the market she felt a familiar lightness in her head. It replaced the roaring and ringing with a bright-white silence and calm.

She walked deep into the market, fast into the frenzy of the maze of tin-roofed stalls. There were dozens of narrow alleyways lined with shacks and sheds, carts and wagons and people calling out. The sweating smell of chicken filled her nostrils; the mustiness of plucked feathers and the dry heat of the coops. She hurried through these smells down another lane of poultry and carcasses of all kinds, desperate to escape the closeness and sad warmth of hanging meat. Though it was part of the market, and she had never wanted to miss one street or alley of it, she found the slaughter overwhelming and ran.

In the market she blended in with the chaos of people and wares. Even at eight a.m. there were vendors who'd been working for two or three hours already. Some of them had already made their best money for the day and were counting wads of bills. A little girl on a tiny chair sat rolling coins in paper tubes. She waved at the Lady Cab Driver, never losing count. Every stall she passed was different from the one next to it. People hung out wind chimes and flags and hand-painted signs advertising deals. Despite the occasional dispute it was an incredibly amiable place, protective. People looked out for one another and still managed to make a living.

Being in the narrow streets again made the Lady Cab Driver feel lost and found at the very same time. I had once been her place of refuge and delight. When her marriage failed, she turned sharply away from all comforts and so turned away from her joyous trips to the market, away from the tight and good-smelling laneways. It was part of an old life, a time when she ran with a loud-laughing crowd who chopped garlic and threw parties and bragged about being red wine alcoholics. She spent a great deal of time in the market back then, buying food for the endless dinner parties she and her husband seemed to have. Her husband was the cook: she was the go-and-get girl. The market was the only place she was allowed to go without him.

When her husband finally informed her that she was no longer loved, she left. She became the Lady Cab Driver who drove nights and slept days and lived uptown, cut off and silent. She slipped away quietly and made no fuss, not wanting to lose her famous composure. She went to live outside the game. In her cab she drove *through* the game, stopping to collect and deliver its many stubborn players, but she never again felt tempted to participate. People in the taxi often asked her opinion on various subjects while she drove. She made a point of changing her opinions on a regular basis to keep herself from believing in any one thing.

There was a spirited gnawing low in her rib cage and she realized that it was hunger. A long-neglected and much-abused stomach that had failed to find anything tantalizing anymore, it now growled and raged at its emptiness. The patches of sunlight and corridors of smell were rousing the deadened sack inside of her. She was starving.

"Hot coffee-cakes! Large! Small!"

"Fresh eggs fresh eggs fresh eggs fresh—" the woman machine gunned the words from her squat position. The Lady Cab Driver stopped to admire the eggs, brown and white and piled in perfect pyramids. She made no connection between the beauty of those eggs and the rank smell of frying she associated with her rented room. The woman seated next to the eggs seemed to know that she had no intention of buying: she simply stopped yelling until the Lady Cab Driver moved away from the display.

"—eggs fresh eggs fresh eggs!" she hammered on, her eyes fixed on the stall across from her own.

A coffee-scented wind blew down the lane and curled around the Lady Cab Driver. She tried not to drink coffee in the morning because it kept her awake. And it had been years since she had consumed anything but dough-nut-shop coffee from paper cups. The smell of beans roasting and being ground made her dizzy and nostalgic. She sought out the source of the perfume. There was a well-built stall to her left that was fronted by huge sacks of coffee beans. A modest sign with carefully painted script read, "The Coffee Lady." As she walked closer to the stall she saw that the woman behind the counter was smiling at her.

"I haven't seen *you* for a long time!" the woman called out. The Lady Cab Driver shook her head. She was sure she had never purchased coffee from this stall before. Perhaps the woman mistook her for someone else.

"Coffee, please," she croaked. Her voice cracked through the words sleepily and she smiled to herself. She had not spoken since three a.m. She hadn't much to say.

"In a mug?" the Coffee Lady grinned, holding out a heavy white ceramic mug.

"Sure," the cabbie answered. The vendor watched her with great interest, a constant smile lurking in the corners of her dark lips. They stood sipping from the steaming hot mugs of coffee, watching two angry women across the alley wrestle with a bag of potatoes.

"I think you miss the market," said the Coffee Lady. She was watching the profile of the Lady Cab Driver.

"It's a good place to think," the Lady Cab Driver nodded, meeting the woman's gaze.

"A nice place to walk," the Coffee Lady added.

The Lady Cab Driver nodded again and turned back to watching the alley while the Coffee Lady rummaged behind the counter. She pulled out a flask and poured a generous amount of the liquid into each of their mugs. When the Lady Cab Driver brought the mug to her lips she smelled brandy and smiled gratefully at the coffee seller. The Coffee Lady was watching something further down the alley with mild alarm. A police officer stood chatting with a vegetable vendor. The Lady Cab Driver's heart began to pound and howl deep in her chest and she set her mug down.

"The market is also a good place to hide," the Coffee Lady said softly. When her nervous customer looked at her questioningly, the Coffee Lady leaned far over the counter, her lips close to the Lady Cab Driver's ear, whispering, "You have blood in your hair."

II

She watched the Coffee Lady's hips and legs move back and forth in lateral slides. It was lunchtime and the market was teeming with people. Everyone wanted coffee: cups of fresh-made, bags of beans. The Lady Cab Driver lay quietly on a bed of burlap coffee-sacks, tucked under the counter where the Coffee Lady banged down mugs of java. After an hour the frenzy subsided and the counter-top was silent again.

"You want another coffee?" the Coffee Lady asked, bending down to retrieve a handful of paper bags from a shelf above the cab driver's head.

"I think I've hit my limit, thanks." Her spine was screaming in its cramped curve, but she needed to smoke more than she needed to stand upright. The Coffee Lady shook her head when the cabbie asked if she could smoke. It wasn't advisable considering the number of police in the market. One of the customers might see the smoke coming out from under the counter and think there was a fire. It was best not to draw attention.

"The market will close down in one hour," whispered the Coffee Lady. She didn't look down as she spoke, "I'll do my usual clean-up and pretend to go home. I leave through the main gate at Saint Street. Two hours later I'll come back, when it's dark. I'll be coming in through a hole in the back of the stall, so don't be frightened. I never light a lamp or candles when I'm in here, I just sit in the dark. I have to ask you to do the same."

Two men came to the counter and the Coffee Lady served them. They were extremely rude and threw their money over the counter. Coins landed in the dust inches from the cab driver's face. She resisted an urge to toss them back up over the counter at the men. The coffee seller knelt down and plucked the coins from the dusty floor and winked at her stall-guest. She could be heard wishing the men a good day.

"You can't let them ruin the day," she said, kneeling down to look deep into the Lady Cab Driver's eyes. There was a sadness in her smile and the cabbie wondered what she had been through in her life. She would have asked but the vendor stood up suddenly and began wiping the grinders down with a chamois cloth.

She talked as she wiped, "I will bring hot empanadas and wine when I come back tonight. I live here, in the stall, but I'm not supposed to. It's against zoning laws, so I sneak in. I'm very careful not to draw attention to myself during the day. I never argue with customers or other vendors. I'm cheerful and patient. At night I have to be silent, and eat quickly so that the food smell doesn't linger. You are welcome to stay for as long as you like, if you like. But this," she paused, struggling to unscrew a part of the grinder, "is a non-smoking hotel. Okay?"

The Lady Cab Driver nodded and felt herself go slightly mad at the thought of perhaps never smoking again.

When the last bolt on the outside of the stall was secured she could sit up straight and stretch her legs out in front of her. Each of her vertebrae flamed as if touched by a match. She stood up and felt obscenely tall in the low-roofed hut. Her head spun from too much coffee and too many pieces of Turkish Delight. The ache of her nicotine addiction made it hard for her to be respectful of the Coffee Lady's request, but she clenched her fists and followed the rules.

She listened to the sounds outside the stall to get an idea of how many people were still moving around the market. Carts wheeled by and people shouted to one another in various languages, wishing each other a good night. In moments she was convinced she was hearing English and then would realize she was hearing a completely foreign tongue. When she was too weak to stand she lay back down on her bed of coffee sacks to await the Coffee Lady's return. Sleep always helped life move a little bit faster.

She awoke to the sound of a man yelling, "Bloody rats! Jesus, look at that one, Freddy!" There was a loud crack, the firing of a gun, and a horrible squealing cry. The men roared victoriously and fired another shot for good measure. Almost next to her head, right outside the stall, a male voice announced:

"I wanna get the *big* one. The King! I wanna see him pop like a water balloon!"

The Lady Cab Driver closed her eyes and shook with silent sobs. A gun cracked again and there was laughter, hunters' laughter that was gleeful in murder. The same cackle she had heard regarding little fat hips. An oniony smell came close to the stall. A good hot fresh smell that made her sit up too fast and crack her head on the underside of the counter.

"Hey, hello! Are you still in there?" the Coffee Lady called softly, working at a latch on the back of the stall.

"Yes, I'm here."

"Empanadas," sang the older woman, handing a paper bag in through a small trapdoor. A bottle followed in a second bag. After some squeezing and grunting the Coffee Lady herself fell into the stall. "Sorry I'm late, there was shooting."

"Open season on the rats," said the cabbie, ripping the bag of food open to let the grand smell out.

"Every night is open season. Poor rats. I don't care about rats. They don't drink coffee."

The two women laughed together and chewed greedily. The Lady Cab Driver washed a mouthful of empanada down with wine and asked, "Can't they just poison them? It seems kind of dangerous to be shooting down a dark street."

There was a gulp in the darkness and the woman said, "No one is supposed to be in here at night. That's how *they* look at it."

"Oh, so anyone who's out on the street after dark gets what they deserve?" The cabbie shook her head in disgust but the darkness of the stall prevented her new friend from seeing the gesture. The white-blonde, the man on the corner: it all came shivering back into the Lady Cab Driver's head.

"The rats are too big to poison. It requires a gun to kill them."

"Or a taxi," the cab driver murmured, hoping she had not been heard. There was a sloshing sound as the coffee vendor poured more wine into their mugs. She leaned close to her guest, chewing and sipping and staring into the blackness.

"Stay here," she finally said, so softly the Lady Cab Driver couldn't be sure she had really heard anything. The woman offered her marketstall as a refuge and the cabbie felt a sudden sweeping loneliness go through her. It was an old feeling of solitary and limited choices.

"But if I stay here too long I'll have to become an official non-smoker," she sighed.

The Coffee Lady giggled, "So you've picked an extreme solution to conquer your addiction."

Later, in a dream within a dream, there were stacks and stacks of oranges, but the oranges were covered in cloves. The smell made her head spin. She was in a locked room with mountains of clove-pierced oranges. The smell made her feel drunk. There was a cat guarding the door of the room and it looked right through her with its yellow-green gaze. She looked at her hands and her fingertips that bled and bled. Apparently she had been the one who pushed the cloves into the oranges. She wasn't sure if she had wanted to or was forced. The smell reminded her of Christmas, a holiday she hated, and she became confused. Then, as though the door hadn't really been locked, she pushed it open and left the room. She stepped into a grey room with nothing in it. The ceiling of the room was thousands of feet above her head. This room had no door, but there were dotted lines on the floor like those painted on a highway, and she became suddenly convinced that a car would come and hit her.

A shot cracked and she awoke sharply with a gasp. She turned to see the Coffee Lady watching her from her mat across the floor.

One morning the Coffee Lady told her, "You have an exceptional heart."

"My exceptional heart needs a cigarette," she replied irritably. She didn't want to seem ungrateful but the desperation she felt was growing. Hiding in the stall had begun to feel less like a refuge and more like a prison. Although she was fed and given wine and asked no questions, and although the Coffee Lady was sweetly maternal, and never warden-like, it was all beginning to frighten her.

That night, when the Coffee Lady was out buying food and waiting for the cover of darkness, the Lady Cab Driver lit a candle and a cigarette. She sat in the warm light and smoked, and felt alive again. She felt justified in her rebellion until the warm food smell came wafting along the back wall of the stall, and then she felt ashamed.

Her host said nothing when she came in and smelled the wax of the snuffed candle and the smell of tobacco ripe and strong in the little room. She laid out the meal and asked the Lady Cab Driver about Tarot cards. When she saw that the piss-bucket was full she cheerfully moved to empty it and the cabbie wanted to scream. This woman took care of everything and never grimaced, never complained. She was content to work and eat and sleep. The cab driver envied her.

At four thirty there was a terrible banging on the tin roof of the stall. Someone was beating on it with a stick. They beat on the thin wooden walls and on the tin again.

"Nobody in there I hope?" a male voice growled through a slit in the wall.

The Coffee Lady lay still on her mat and the cabbie held her breath.

A man's voice far away screamed, "I got the King! Yeee-hawww!"

The nearer voice said, "Missus Coffee? Helloooo?" The man belonging to the voice began banging again until another series of shots rang out and his footsteps indicated that he had run down the road, away from the stall, at last.

The Coffee Lady rolled over on her side, facing away from the Lady Cab Driver. When the time came to open the stall in the morning she was cheerful, rummaging in a sack. She pulled out a book and handed it to the cab driver.

"I brought you something to read," she announced proudly. "I meant to give it to you last night but I was upset about the smoking."

The cabbie turned the book over and over in her hands and said, "Thanks. I'm really sorry I let you down. I think I should probably leave here."

Turning from her task the coffee seller stared at her guest with wide eyes, "Sometimes we're allowed to get away with things in this life. It isn't necessary to be punished for every mistake we make. I understand why you did what you did."

"I wonder if you know what I've done," said the cab driver. She pretended to study the cover of the book.

"No. I don't know. But I forgive you in advance," the woman laughed.

"You're a saint."

The Coffee Lady shook her head, "Oh, no. I could never claim sainthood." She pointed to the book and said, "I read these poems in a very black time." And she went out to crank up the awning while the Lady Cab Driver opened the book to a page marked with a slip of paper:

His vision, from the constantly passing bars,
has grown so weary that it cannot hold
anything else. It seems to him there are
a thousand bars, and behind the bars, no world.

"Oh hello," she heard the Coffee Lady say flatly. They were open for business, but the first customer was obviously an unwelcome one.

"Payable immediately," the voice said.

"I was repairing my grinder," the Coffee Lady explained, shuffling her feet in the dust on the floor. It stirred up a cloud in front of where the cabbie hid.

"The fine doubles every time you're caught to a maximum of three times. Then we close you down permanently. One-twenty-five up front. Please."

The Coffee Lady was furious, "Look, I have to repair my equipment when it breaks down! I'm not sleeping here, I'm working. I refuse to pay!"

The voice said, "We can shut you down today if you'd rather."

She banged a fist down on the counter-top, "I maintain that I was here fixing the equipment that I use to make a living and that I have every right to do so when it is convenient to me. I'm a businesswoman."

The man sighed heavily, "We smelled food and tobacco, lady."

"You go and tell every person working in this market that they can't eat a little something while they're working! Go and tell them that they can't smoke a cigarette while they wait for customers to come along! I was working. I eat when I work! I smoke when I work! I even *breathe* when I work! Go away with your little ticket pad and find someone who is really doing something wrong."

By this time the woman was red-cheeked and stamping.

"I'll review your complaint," the voice said. "However, I must insist that you not bring food in here after hours while you are *working* because it attracts the rats that we are spending thousands of dollars to get rid of!"

The Coffee Lady threw her head back and roared, "Go tell Hartman to carry his dead fish home with him every night! Tell Hague to drive all his cheeses home in his car and bring them back every morning! I don't bring rats into the market with one sandwich! Crazy!"

When the man had gone, the Coffee Lady looked down at the Lady Cab Driver curled up on the floor at her feet and whispered, "I learned to argue in prison. It has come in very handy."

III

The Coffee Lady wondered if she should hire her cab-driving friend to be her Saturday assistant. It would allow the Lady Cab Driver the divine privilege of standing upright in daylight once a week, and the Coffee Lady needed the help. It was a risky proposal, and though one couldn't lay on the floor of a marketstall forever, the cabbie didn't want to be seen or recognized. Perhaps no one had noticed the taxi on the ramp, but perhaps someone had. Confrontations with the police were of no interest to either woman. The Lady Cab Driver was becoming fearful of the world outside the stall and her generous host was unable to decide what the best solution was.

"Go for a walk," said the Coffee Lady, sifting her hands through freshly roasted and still-warm coffee beans. "I need a minute to think."

"Do you want me to leave, for good?"

"No. I've gotten attached to the idea of you being here. I like stepping over you while I work. I like eating with you at night and talking to you about things. And I don't like liking all that. Give me a few minutes, okay?"

The Lady Cab Driver understood. She would have given almost anything to be back on her sofa, sipping gin and smoking through holes in blankets. Those rituals had become a far-off history she could never have back. Not with any ease.

"Go," the coffee seller said, "go and read your Rilke book somewhere else for awhile."

The Lady Cab Driver stepped onto the pavement and shivered. She walked until she lost herself in the wilderness of the textiles section of the market. Swathes of bright cloth billowed on clotheslines hung over the street. Customers could point to a certain fabric and a woman would come along with a hooked pole and pull it down for inspection. It seemed as though everyone who passed the cabbie jangled with jewelry. There were buckets of boots and towers of hats. A barrel held buttons of all shapes and sizes: these were sold at a dollar a pound. She pushed through a forest of saris, then through a tight jungle of cotton and silk and leather. She was hoping to push her way back to the street where the spice vendors and bakers kept shop. She wanted bread and curry and doughnuts.

Rounding a corner, she found herself in a wide lane. The asphalt was covered with a slick of bloody crushed ice and fish-rot. The smell assaulted her and she put her hands up to cover her nose and mouth. Holding her breath she stepped over guts and cast-away fish heads; men and women in aprons laughed as she slipped on discarded bits of scale and skin. To fend off the stench she wrapped her hair around her face like a veil, but there was none of her perfume left on the curls, only a thick reek of coffee.

Stumbling down tighter lanes, she felt as though she would never find the Coffee Lady's stall again. Now she was in the vegetable sellers' row; nothing looked familiar though she had been there many times before. She walked more slowly and tried to calm herself, watched for familiar lanes or corner shops that would jog her memory. The ringing in her ears returned and its thundering leaked down from her head and into her heart. Dropping the handfuls of hair away from her face, she sniffed for the Coffee Lady's stall. There were still so many police in the market! To look lost would seem suspicious, and she held her head high in false confidence. The sun bore down and made her squint and trip over unseen crates and litter.

She saw the stall that was Home and ran toward it, shading her eyes. Three police officers were holding the Coffee Lady; one was snapping handcuffs roughly around her thin wrists while another grabbed her hair and yelled loudly in her face. The Lady Cab Driver felt herself falling to the ground, felt something biting into her arms. Cold metal rings were snapped around her own wrists and she was dragged up from the ground. The Coffee Lady smiled at her as she was dragged away by the brutish officers of Law, down a lane leading to the gate at Saint Street.

IV

Out of a Tanqueray mist Kathleen Deluth can see the alarm clock on the coffee table. Time for work. She heaves herself out from under the afghan blanket and knocks an ashtray to the floor on her way to the kitchen. Standing next to the fridge she rubs her head, tries to brush her wild red hair out of her clotted eyes. It occurs to her...

The rat is still there on the kitchenette floor, bloody and stiff. She had chosen to kill it rather than chase it out of the apartment. Why? When she opened the cupboard it had come at her with its teeth flashing, the biggest rodent she had ever seen. Still, her memory of losing her temper was fuzzy, clouded by the extra-tall glass of gin she downed after working all night. Her last fare in the taxi had been a real prick, a nut. He criticized her driving, her clothes, all women in all capacities. And there was something odd about his destination. When he mentioned surprising his ex-girlfriend at three a.m. she kicked him out of the cab and came home to discover the rat in her kitchen. Thus the extra-tall Tanq.

She grabs the dust-pan and a garbage bag and tries to scoop up the dead rat. A shiver runs down her spine: his bloody stiffness stirs her blurred memory. She dumps its corpse into the bag and throws it onto the fire escape, eager to get rid of it.

On the sofa she sits with a mug of coffee and a cigarette. She feels a curious aching emptiness inside her, as though something or someone is missing. Her thoughts turn to the rat again, whose murder she tries to justify with recollections of its terrifying smile. The face of the creep in her taxi fills her head, his provocative words and unsettling smile.

"You scare me, you pay," she says aloud, butting out her cigarette with exaggerated force. And she decides that she will not pay attention to the world squealing on the street below, nor take notice of the bag of coffee beans sitting on top of the TV. She will get in her cab and do her best to notice as little as possible.

The cab, however, is not parked in the lot outside Kathleen's building. Its bloodied bumpers are being swabbed by gloved investigators on a northbound exit-ramp out of the city.

Madame Frye

Dip dip dip and dunk bloody dunk. I'm so sick of it: the stink of it, the swing of it from batterbowl to fryer. The sing of it hitting the oil. Fed right up and pissed right off. I hate every perfect white piece, every snowy slab. I hate the chips, the mushy peas, the buckets of coleslaw: all of it. I've been sick of it since the beginning; so much and for so long that hating has become a way of life.

To think I could've been a hand-model! That I could have made my fortune in lotion advertisements or showing off gloves, or been found waving my perfect fingers in a jewellery shop, promoting the potential glamour of diamonds! There's a jeweller right across the street. Every time I lift the steel shutter in the mornings I see the shop: Zucker's Gems. He surely wouldn't have me now, Mr. Zucker wouldn't. My perfect fingers are no longer so perfect, are they? Look, they've grown all ruddy and burnt from handling the fish and the chips and the newsprint. There's hardly a hope of me becoming a model for anything now. I've no one to blame but myself.

I married *him*. The once-king of fish 'n chips. Wasn't he Mister Proud and Successful when I met him? Didn't he talk me into standing here on the tiles, just two days a week, love, just three or four afternoons? And not long after that he announced his *depression* and flopped down on the sofa for good. *Depressed* he calls himself! Oh, but he's never so down that he can't swing a fist up in displeasure. Never so dispirited that he can't find the energy to complain. There's an awful lot wrong with the world from where he sits. And most of it has some connection to me. There's precious little about me that he finds satisfactory. Whereas I simply let him be himself, a miserable sod, the arse I was foolish enough to marry, he can't give me the same. He's quick to point out my declining beauty while avoiding mirrors himself, and equally concerned about my intellect though he can barely find his way through the TV guide.

It's not martyrdom that keeps me here, nor love. It's my daughter Penn. She's far too young to cope with my departure. And when I go I plan to go alone, without anyone who needs me. Since she's still a tender fifteen, I've no choice but to stay on behind this counter. I won't have any part in the breaking of her heart; she'll have plenty of chances to have it bruised by the whims of the world at large. What goes on in our household is certainly no worse than the goings-on outside the door of Frye's. At least here one knows just what kind of misery to expect.

PENNY

I pray for Mum every night after we close up the shop. It isn't easy to pray in this house, what with Duh sitting up all night in front of the television. He's taken up crying, you see, and the combined bleating of the TV and wailing of Duh makes it difficult to pursue one's faith. Mum has no idea that I'm as religious as I am. In fact I think she assumes I'm like any teenager, faithless and bored. There are certain expectations that go along with being young. One of them is that one has to be dumb and in need of guidance. The other is that sex and matters of it are a complete mystery.

Well, I've never been dumb. And I designed my own personal religion at the age of twelve, a faith that has never let me down. But telling Mum that I pray to gods of my own creation might be a bit much for her. Religion is an extremely private matter, after all.

As for the matter of sex being a mystery, it's not. For example, I know that my Mum should never have married my Duh. This is the problem with the age-old tradition of mums marrying before they have children. It's a useless trend. If only they would refrain from selecting a mate until the children arrived to counsel them on the choice, everyone would be happier. My Mum shouldn't have married at all, you see, but she went ahead and did so before I could tell her *Don't!* And if I'd been around I would most definitely kept her from marrying Duh. Or anyone.

You see, I know things about Mum that she doesn't know about herself. It makes my life rather frustrating at times. I rely heavily on my religion to help me through it all. It's a combination of Jungian psychology and Satanic ritual and borrows heavily from Wiccan witchcraft as well. I devised it based on extensive and varied readings done in the loo from ages eight to twelve. My study continues, but the foundations of my faith are quite in place.

My primary god (there are 3 in total, plus thirteen sub-gods) has instructed me to pray for Mum on a nightly basis. According to the dictates of my faith I must work quietly and slowly with a focused mind. Last week I concentrated on praying that Mum could win a trip. She's forever entering sweepstakes in hopes of winning vacations. But now I've abandoned that prayer in favour of a much more practical one:

Mighty gods, please help my Mum to realize her potential, even in the face of constant nit-picking from my Duh. Let her run the chip shop proudly and let her notice that she has an admirer in her midst, one who may even love her.

For myself I say the following prayer:

Mighty gods, please let Frye's Fish 'n Chips become the target of political terrorism so that I may cease reeking of halibut.

NAN

I remember the last things that impressed me: the furnaces here. And the lack of damp. Those two things were enough to drive me to marriage! I was young after all, and obviously chilled enough to be moved by good heating. I wanted to live in this country. Marriage was the fastest way to achieve that. So it wasn't that my head was filled with fancies of romance: it was filled with visions of immigration and a warm sitting room.

* * *

He wanted me to help him in the shop. Business was booming, he said, he couldn't manage it on his own. Now that he's on the sofa bed twenty hours a day he feels it is less than booming. Since I took over, he says, it hasn't been doing very well. The truth is, business is even better. The place is clean and efficient, two things he'd never notice. And we bring in a very nice sum each and every day. Is it my fault if I forget to ring in the odd order?

It's his depression that makes me do it. Skim the odd fiver. He's rarely *healthy* enough to look at the books, and even when he does look there's nothing out of sorts. Because despite his low opinion of my intelligence I'm brilliant at mathematics. Besides, he doesn't pay me, not a real wage. The roof over my head is supposed to be sufficient payment. Penny gets paid half of what her friends make in clothing shops. I've told her to get a mall-job but she won't. She's afraid of her Duh I think, and who wouldn't be, what with him swinging his fists every time he gets angry. He's never hit her, I've made sure of that. And he seems to prefer me as a target. I just wish she'd work elsewhere, away from the grease and oil. Though she swears she has no interest in boys or romance I'm afraid her complexion prevents her from socializing. She's got the worst case of spots I've ever seen, and it's all from being around the fryer.

He's hardly a bother anymore. In a coma from the time the morning chat-shows come on the TV 'til at least eight at night. He puts in a full day of depression seven days a week, goes dutifully to the sofa like a worker to a factory. When he's not on one of his crying jags he's quite unobtrusive. I just have to keep his beer fridge full, a fine art given his appetite for drink. Extending the hours of the shop was the smartest thing I ever did. It keeps me out of the flat for at least twelve hours, if not longer. And when Penn comes in I run to the beer shop and replenish his stock. There's hardly ever a glitch in my system unless he devises one. Maybe I've just gotten used to everything, even the smell of his knuckles on unhappy days.

He's been out of my sexual favour since Penny came along, and on that front he doesn't bother to bully. Romantic ambitions don't run in his family just as divorce doesn't run in mine. I've never peered through the branches of my family tree to hunt for examples of tragedy amongst the happily married ladies and gentlemen who've been Greers. Now that I'm a Frye I suppose I could plead unbearable misery, but for what ? The little money I've tucked away is for Penn's college. After she's off to school I'll start saving up for Bora Bora.

It's hot in Bora Bora and I imagine they've no need to impress anyone with their furnaces there.

In the Spice House

PENNY

I've realized that Mum is at a crucial point. Despite the fact that she has given up entirely on the idea of enjoying life, she still has passion. I've seen her lose her temper with the man who brings the boxes of fish. There's fire in her somewhere. It's only Duh who makes her weak-willed. If she can still scream at the Halibut Man like that there's no telling when she'll finally snap with Duh.

Mighty gods, please give my Mum the power to push my Duh's head into the deep-fryer next time he comes into the shop. I pray to you so that you might inspire him to leave the sofa and check on the business.

Mum is suspicious because I've asked to work more hours in the shop. But I think she's tired enough to let me run things more often. I've told her that I need the money, which isn't true; my only expenses are candles and the odd yard of silk. I save the rest of my money in a cigar box. It's all part of my plan to bundle Mum off to someplace hot. Given my wages I think something more drastic will have to happen to boost financing. One of my sub-gods suggested the prayer about Mum shoving Duh in the fryer. I'm allowed to question their ordinances, and that suggestion seemed risky to me. But I prayed for it anyway, that Mum will just go mad and murder Duh one of these days.

Unfortunately for Mum, even a good reason like having endured life with my Duh wouldn't allow her any forgiveness in a court of Law. Judges love to send people like Mum to jail. And I want to get her out of a prison, not get her thrown into a new one. Perhaps another sort of prayer is needed...

In the Spice House

If I was a spiritual person I might find this work very comforting. The repetition, the simplicity, the very consistent nature of fish 'n chip rhythms. I suppose the problem is that I mastered it long ago and I take no joy in my mastery. There's a shortage of delight in this place, that's certain. From the most optimistic standpoint, I enjoy talking to some of the customers. The ones that don't know *him*. Most of the people I serve are my customers, but there's a pack of Old Boys who've been coming in forever. Like him, they exist for the pleasures of a pint. I suspect not one of them has ever been in his own kitchen. From Frye's to the Gold Crow and back to Frye's again for supper.

There's one who reminds me of *him* most. Mister Forester. He wears his hair combed over his greasy bald skull in a sideways accident of the comb, sweater tight across his big belly. He's a belligerent old sod, as unsmiling as they come, and rude as the day is long. Grabs at his change, pays in handfuls of coin, a real prize of a man. It's my deepest hope that he's a bachelor; no woman should have to tolerate his innate hostility. And of course he comes in twice daily, never missing a meal.

Today as I wrapped his chips in the cone of paper he insists upon, I smiled to myself, thinking of the scene of his demise. A great whopping attack of the heart no one knew he had. That's the most likely scenario given his diet. What a tremble the earth would make if he hit the pub floor! The only reason I allowed myself to fancy it in such detail was that he earned my malice.

"Poor Jimmy," he said as I handed him his change.

"Eh?" I asked, not sure why he was bringing up Jimmy at all. I rarely call my husband by his Christian name and it takes me off guard when others do.

"I said *Poor Jimmy*. Are you losing your hearing old

gal?" He rocked on his heels and looked completely pleased with himself.

I shouldn't have bothered to venture further into it with him, but I did, asking, "What's so poor about Jimmy?"

He shook his head and stuffed three or four chips into his gob at once, and with the chewed muck fully exposed said, "He's got himself a dog of a bride, hasn't he? Poor, poor Jim. Oh well, not my worry. See you at supper!"

The Old Boys are all the same, but he's the only one who goes out of his way to infuriate me. He knows Jim doesn't do battle over anyone's honour but his own, that he can say whatever he pleases. I wish that most of these old buggers would drop off and give me a little peace, but not as keenly as I wish *that* one would.

PENNY

It's an extract of spider-belly that explodes at the top of the stomach. High enough in the gut and low enough in the oesophagus that it mimics a heart attack. I've mixed it with a little sleeping powder to delay its inevitable violence. Without the sleeping powder it would kill instantly, which won't do since lots of them eat right in the shop at the window-counter. In a mixed formula it sits in the belly for a bit and isn't active 'til it eats through the guck of batter. The flour and egg help to slow it as well, which buys a great deal of time.

Part of my faith requires that I develop a skill with chemistry. And, as history has proven, chemistry has both a good and bad side. I believe that poisons are a natural part of the universe and are thus not subject to the descriptive word *evil.* There is no crime in eliminating unpleasantness from the world. At this time I am a bedroom chemist, limited to the poor facilities of my room and held back by inadequate access to the proper poisons. Some day I hope to live in a large flat where I will devote an entire room to the scientific pursuits of my religion.

The theory of my mixture is sound, but as is the way with all experiments, it must be tested on a subject. Luckily, I work alone in the shop this evening. Mum's off to do the shopping, and her absence affords me the opportunity to test out a quantity of batter.

But who shall I test it on? I've a vague knowledge of the sorts of people who treat Mum poorly, but it would be best, in the event that the mixture succeeds, if it were tested on someone *deserving*. Someone truly evil. The word *evil* is handy when describing a bastard, as well as being delicious to mutter under one's breath.

NAN

I'm worried about Penn. She keeps to herself so much; always in her room with the door locked. I hear pages flipping and drawers opening and closing. She studies for such long hours, way into the night, and yet she doesn't do very well at school. Given her genetics it's no surprise that she struggles: *he's* certainly not a secret genius, and I was never much for actually attending my classes. When she's not in her room she's hanging 'round the shop, asking to work more often. If she quits school I'll never forgive myself. I've hardly a spare minute to help her with her studies and she never asks. Not for help or advice. Our conversations revolve around the shop, the weather. On rare occasions she asks about England, but generally she's quiet. And, though I'm chatty in my head, I've grown rather silent myself. Maybe she's talkative at school, amongst her friends. I assume she has friends, though none ever come by the shop to visit.

But why *would* she have friends? It's possible she doesn't understand the concept, given her parentage. There've been no cocktail parties here, no gatherings of couples. *His* closest friends live inside the television and mine are waiting for me in the South Pacific. Since Penn doesn't watch TV and doesn't appear to read novels, I'm terribly afraid she lives full-time in the real world. That can't be good for anyone. If I didn't live part of my life in fantasy I'd be lost. I'm careful to indulge in the odd novel along with my geographic research. But, since all my books are hidden away, how could she follow my escapist example?

After I've been to the library tonight I think I'll ask Penny to have tea with me in the shop. There's no way to have tea anywhere else: the flat is *his* kingdom. To sit in the kitchenette is to be within his earshot. One avoids the kitchen at night unless one wishes to become his on-call waitress. His *depression* makes it difficult for him to fetch his own beer, affecting his legs as it does. He had a burst of wellness that allowed him to rig up an intercom from sofa to shop so that I could be beckoned in any moment of need. You can imagine how distracting it is to be mid-fry in the store and hear that buzzer going off.

He taught me the system:

One long buzz means *More beer.* One short buzz means *Turn the channel on the TV.* Two quick buzzes means *Ready for my supper.* A series of staccato buzzes means *I've run out of beer completely.*

Not one of the buzzes includes a *please, love* or a *would you mind?*

So, after I've collected my books at the library, I'll come back to the shop and help Penn with the clean-up. And we'll have a cup of tea at the window-counter together. It's been far too long since we had a real chat. I'm not sure how it will go off, since I've nothing but questions to ask her. She's been saddled with a rather outwardly dull Mum. I could never tell her about Bora Bora, after all, since it would only inspire anxiety in her heart about my taking off.

PENNY

Mighty gods, the decision has been made. Give the poison your blessing and let it work. Send me a sign that it has worked, some report of its success. Mum's off at the library again, so you must help me in this limited but very powerful time.

Oh but he's greasy and perverse, a real lizard. Asked me how old I am and squeezed my fingers when I handed him his change. But it wasn't his offense to me that helped me make the decision. He slighted Mum. And when you slander the name of the Matriarch, you sin against my church. He said, "You're much lovelier than that old Mum of yours. Must get your good looks from Jimmy."

Well, dear sir, *Jimmy* is nothing but ugliness, and to imply my resemblance to him was a very big mistake. My *old Mum* is the most beautiful woman on earth. I'm afraid you'll have to do penance. Kneel before chemistry, you bastard!

NAN

Tea went off extremely well. Penny was delighted by my appearance in the shop and insisted on making the tea. Apparently she's developed a taste for herbal tea and wanted me to try some. It was wonderful stuff, a very relaxing beverage with a peculiar sweet flavour and strong smell, like autumn leaves or something. And chatty! She asked me dozens of questions, blotting out my opportunity to ask her any. What was I like when I was a young girl? What was my Mum like? My Dad? Her curiosity about my family was unbridled. Since I rarely think of childhood it was difficult to remember the details she was after. But she got me talking, and it wasn't long before the bloody buzzer went off.

"He's a misery," said Penn, staring straight ahead out the window of the shop. Her eyes, when she turned them back to me, were flat and hard. Her voice was equally passionless, as though she was simply announcing a fact.

"That he is. But you won't have to put up with him forever, lovey," I consoled her, about to tell her about the grand prospects of her adult future, but she cut me off.

"You're right," she said loudly. And she squeezed my hand absentmindedly. When she pumped my fingers I noticed the tattoo, but the buzzer went off, a ceaseless long buzz that screamed and screamed and meant only one thing to me.

You're in for it, woman.

PENNY

Even though I feel like my knowledge of Mum is purely philosophical, I love her to pieces. And when she came into the shop tonight wanting tea, with me, I knew that magic was at work and that I had made a very wise decision. The air rippled with god-like energy. I felt I didn't have to hide my interest in her at all. There are so many things, basic things, I've wanted to ask her. Nothing too private, of course, just historical facts. I've been wondering who she was before the blight that is my Duh came upon her.

The buzzer went long and angry-sounding. If I were her I'd have locked myself in the shop. She's done it before, slept by the fryer with the bolt secured. I know because I've heard him pounding in the night, and the next morning the kettle's been cold on the stove, meaning she never had her tea. But tonight she went into the flat, dragging her satchel of books with a weary smile on her face.

There was a round of his usual shouting and slamming, though it didn't last for nearly as long. The magic must be on.

NAN

I live in a lagoon. My hut is small with a huge verandah overlooking the water. Everything is bright blue, soft brown, brilliantly striped and patterned. My every day begins at earliest dawn, but I don't get out of bed and move into the cold white of the chip shop. There's no fryer to be turned on, no coleslaw to be made up. I drink coffee instead of tea and there is no other human voice slicing through the morning. Birds cry, the water roars against the rocks below, and I ease into each day as though I was the most perfect human alive. I weave, as taught by the village women, and go to lunch at a cafe where I drink cold punch, eat fresh-caught fish that is still sweet from the sea. Or maybe I don't eat fish at all...

In the afternoon I go down the long dusty road that curls toward the water. She sits there on a striped blanket, her skin chocolate against the pale sand. Without a word we go to the water and swim for hours. And when we are streched out on the warm blanket she rests her hand on my hip and smiles with her eyes closed. And she whispers Thank-you *and I never know why.*

She's the only one who comes into the shop and says "Thank-you" as though she means it. Her skin isn't chocolate yet, though it's certainly olive and would tan to a beautiful cocoa colour if it had the opportunity of sunshine. I'm not sure if she says thank-you for the fish or if she's thanking me for the poems that I wrap inside the newsprint. In any case she returned to the shop after I put the first poem in. Of course it was only Wordsworth, very tame, but it didn't turn her off. And she's stuck it out through bolder bits: Auden and even Dylan Thomas. She's never said a word about the poems, just *Thank-you.*

But she came in today and, after I handed her the package of fish, she said, quiet so that the man eating in the window couldn't hear, "I don't mean to sound ungrateful, but do you know any *female* poets?"

I blushed like a beet and didn't say a word, couldn't. And right after she left the shop I drifted back to Bora Bora and burnt the next three orders to a crisp.

Today I woke up with a welted cheek and a black heart. He *spared me* the full treatment I suppose, being too drunk to make his complete virility known. But because today is a Tuesday I forgot about my misery for awhile. She comes in Tuesdays and Fridays, and she makes *him* go away for awhile. It's me who should be thanking, but I can't manage it, so I put the poems in her orders of fish.

He's always telling me I'm sneaky. And so I am.

PENNY

Mighty gods, give me a sign! Let me know that my experiment worked so that I may journey further in my work. My world is still imperfect. Send me a signal!

Mum was in such an odd mood when I popped into the shop afterschool. All dreamy. Perhaps the tea never left her system. It *was* a tranquilizing tea, but I doubt that it would hang about in her bloodstream for that long. Maybe her admirer has come forth! That's probably too much to ask of the gods just yet. One can't expect them to look after everything all at once.

There was a huge quantity of burnt fish in the garbage pail. Mum never ruins a piece of fish, even out of spite. No doubt the old ogre on the sofa buzzed her all day long and she forgot about the fryer. But it's strange: she's in such a fine mood. Mum's rarely grumpy, even despite the conditions in which she lives, but neither is she ever *happy*. She even had the radio on, something Duh forbids since it might prevent her from hearing the buzzer. But she had it on, and quite loud, a cheerful station that plays International Music in the afternoons.

"Bonjour!" she said when I came in. What? I'm beginning to think that Mum is suffering some kind of splitting of her personality. She asked me if I'd mind working the next afternoon and would I mind terribly about missing school! Apparently there's a funeral she has to attend with Duh. She said it so pleasantly and seemed almost happy to go, even with Duh for company.

Mighty gods, please don't let my Mum go mad in any way that involves her trying to love my Duh again. I can't bear any further aberrations just now.

I rarely pray in the presence of others but today I had to say a quick one right there in the shop. Mum was busy at the fryer, *humming* even. But, as always, the gods were good to me and delivered a quick explanation.

"Whose funeral?" I asked, a bit frantically, prompted by the urgings of sub-god number six.

"That old Mister Forester. Had a heart attack. Hope his family doesn't try to sue us for serving the old glutton!" And still her voice was cheery, but at least I could see, by way of the vague guilt in her eyes, that she was happy about his death, and not so much about spending the day with Duh. "I won't be allowed to attend the wake, so I'll be back for the evening shift, okay? Then you'll be free to wander off."

Allowed! It sickens me to the marrow that my Mum can even think of life in terms of allowance and disallowance. But at least she doesn't appear to be falling in some kind of weird half-love with my Duh.

Mighty gods, primary and sub, thank you for killing Mister Forester. He needn't have criticized the beauty of my strange and mysterious Mum.

NAN

My greatest comfort sitting here amongst these husbands (and wives where there are wives) is that I'll be sent home after the ceremony. And it's a good thing, too, because the eulogies are endless it seems. Tricky old Forester! One would never have suspected him of being such a fine fellow. He's fondly remembered by his comrades from the pub. Jimmy sits next to me shuddering and blubbering as though he's lost his twin brother. All the men weep, including the minister, but then he looks like he's already been to the pub. After this interminable festival of grievous praise they'll all go off to the Gold Crow and get blind drunk. It must be a big day for Jimmy; his first social jaunt in months. The last time he managed to leave his beloved sofa was on the occasion of his friend Geoffrey's divorce party. He came home weaving and teasing me with the promise of divorce.

I wonder, do I look as tired as the other women? They've all got the look of worn-down shoes, slumping over their handbags, sagging under the weight of heavily sprayed hair. For all my weakness I've never stooped to hairspray, never relied on the sad crutch of excessive cosmetics. Jimmy can say what he likes about my diminishing beauty. A quick glance in any mirror would tell him *he's* lost his princely air.

Hard to believe that I once considered him *handsome*. But what does that mean in a man? I suppose it means he had a way about him. What *was* it that I found so attractive? Despite my desire to immigrate there was *something* that appealed, something I found tolerable. I think it was his eyes. When we met they were big and blue, the icy azure type that can't be read. That was long ago, when simple things still fascinated me. Oh, his eyes are still a *kind* of blue, but they aren't the same. Any brilliance they possess comes from the monstrous combination of original blue against jaundice-yellow with scarlet highlights. And as for them being unreadable, well, that mystery's been solved.

I've drifted off. Jimmy pinches my arm to get my attention. Everyone around us has risen to leave the church.

"Off to the Crow," he announces. There's not a shred of mourner in him now. The promise of a free pint has him grinning. It seems the penny-pinching Forester made allowances in his will for a binge. I wondered why there were no flowers. Jimmy keeps motioning for me to hurry up.

"Have a nice time at the wake," I mumble.

"You're coming along," he tells me, and pushes me through the crowd of guffawing men. "Gotta get a seat at the Crow. I'm not standing all night."

Doesn't he push the horror all the further! Putting his arm around me in the pub in a pantomime of lovey-dove, ordering me a *shandy*. And, when I return to the table from calling poor Penn, doesn't he claim to have *missed* me! It's all I can do to keep from retching my lunch, wedged in next to him and surrounded by his cronies, me playing the good wife.

When I called Penn she didn't sound upset about having to run the shop 'til closing hour. All she said was, "Good luck, Mum."

PENNY

It worked! Forester dropped without any suspicion. The only sad part about the whole thing was that Mum had to attend the funeral with Duh. And the wake! Poor Mum.

Mum's admirer came in today. She looked surprised to see *me* behind the counter, even a little disappointed. I put an extra piece of fish in her order just to let her know she's being well looked after in Mum's absence. But then a queer thing happened: she came back in half an hour and looked even more disappointed. I asked her was there a problem with her fish, and she said No, nothing wrong with the fish. Then she became quite nervous and flushed.

"I didn't get my poem," she said. I had no idea what she was talking about. "There's supposed to be a poem wrapped around the fish."

It never occurred to me that she might be mad as a hatter. I always thought she was quite original, wearing men's suits and doing her hair with pomade. But when she started going on about poems in her fish and asking me if I was a new employee when she's seen me before, working next to Mum on occasion... It troubles me. The last thing Mum needs is *another* nutter in her life. Duh's been plenty to worry about for one lifetime.

Eventually she left the shop. But I can't figure out what on earth she was going on about. Could it be that her affection for Mum has made her delusional? Or is it that she's just naturally stark raving?

Mightiest of the gods: please surround my Mum with a protective spell. Her admirer may very well be a crazy lady. Something in Mum's soul could be causing her to attract madness. I fear that her life will be filled with lunatics unless she is protected. And please, if you will it, allow me to escape a similar Fate.

In the Spice House

NAN

I know so little about my own mum.

This occurred to me today in the shop. Not only because I left my parents behind along with my country. It's older than that, my ignorance. What made me think of it was Penn. How she drilled me with questions the one night and now seems content with our usual silence. We drift past each other in the shop, exchanging the most superficial words. There haven't been any more questions from her and God knows I find it an effort to ask *her* any. My mum rarely asked me questions about anything but school and sex. Was I smart? Was I *active?* That's how she said it, too, no subtle leading up to the subject, just, "Are you *active* yet?" I can't imagine asking Penny such a thing! It'd horrify the poor girl.

My mum *must've* had her own secret thoughts and feelings, must *now*. I'm afraid I'm continuing the family tradition of being estranged and ignorant. There was never an opportunity for me to ask my Mum the deeper questions. I just assumed she was Mum; content to be, satisfied and happy. I never fancied that she might have had dreams about running away from us or wishes that went unfulfilled. I was too busy planning my escape from England to ask. Now I wish I had inquired.

Perhaps I'll write Penny a letter listing off all the things she might like to know about me. Like the lists in magazines, you know, '101 Things You Wanted To Know About Mum But Were Afraid To Ask,' that sort of thing. Maybe she'd feel inspired to do the same for me and then we'd be closer. But then, maybe growing closer isn't a good idea, given my eventual plans. No matter where I go I'll always be her Mum. I'll just be a little hard to get to.

There's plenty my mum doesn't know about *me*. She'd have asked by now if she felt concerned. When I sent her my wedding photo she wrote me a card that said, "He seems like a lovely boy." No doubt she still envisions Jimmy as that lovely boy, and why should she imagine anything else? I'm not in the habit of ringing her up to say, "He's a bad-tempered sod, drinks too much, claims he's *depressed*." I'd have quite the phone bill if I called her up about every bruise and insult.

I laughed myself silly at the thought of ringing her up and saying, "Mum, are *you* active?" But then it disgusted me to think of it and I began thinking about which poem I should copy out next.

Perhaps it's just the way of mothers and daughters, the quiet pact of mutual ignorance. I shouldn't let it trouble me so much if I'm not prepared to remedy the situation with Penn. Where knowing my own mum is concerned it's probably a lost cause as well. All sentiment and no action, that's what I am.

PENNY

Mum's problem is that she's a Taurus. If she were a Gemini she'd have fled by now. She's stuck as a stick behind this counter. I watch her with the customers, her cheerful, resigned way. A stick of dynamite wouldn't move her from this misery. It's a terrible tragedy. With her looks! I see the way men look at her sometimes. They notice how lovely she is, but then they think of her as the Frye's lady. She has the advantage of looking good with greasy hair; it hangs in little ringlets around her face where certain strands escape her pony-tail. Not me. I have the eternal cross to bear: I look just like Duh. His eyes, his pink skin, the same turdish hair. He doesn't look at all like a Pisces should. There's nothing poetic about him. Why on earth a woman as beautiful as my Mum would ever have chosen him escapes me.

In the Spice House

The only thing that has saved me on this planet is that I am a Scorpio. We're the best of the zodiacal positions: psychic, sharp-tongued, yet powerfully silent. The kids at school can't figure me out; no one can. Scorpios have a pre-natal understanding of revenge. Even the most passing comment contains information that is useful to us. There is *nothing* that we miss, and when we choose to strike we never lose. Mister Forester, for example. I don't waste my energy being nice to people I can't stand, I just observe them quietly. They don't even suspect my dislike. And then I get even.

But Mum. Everything about her way with Duh screams hatred. She's far too obvious. That's why he doesn't respect her: she hates him but she doesn't take action. If I was married to my Duh I'd have killed him by now; lured him into the bedroom and murdered him in the sheets. I'd have strangled him with my bare hands after his first display of violence. And yet... perhaps Mum had me for a reason. Because I'm sure Duh hit her before I arrived on the scene. But she's been waiting for *something*. Perhaps the whole reason she decided to have a baby with that bastard is so that she could have an ally.

I tell you, there is no ally like a Scorpio.

"Mum," I say. There are no customers in the shop. We are wiping the salt shakers for the tenth time today because people always press them against the fish and get them gucky. It's a job we do together because we both *hate* it. Quite often we swear under our breath as we wipe, and it's our one act of complete togetherness. But today I want to use our communal time to give her a hint. "Mum, do you know what it means to be a Scorpio?"

"Yeah, you're one, aren't you?" she says, unscrewing the lid on one of the shakers. Someone has put a cigarette butt in the salt.

I utter a profanity and return to my orginal line of

thought, "Yes I am. But do you know anything about the signs?"

She smiles, "Just what I read in magazines, you know, the 'Bedtime Guide To Love.' Do they teach astrology in school now? That'd be fun."

Risking a revelation, I fold my arms across my chest and shake my head No. "I study it on my own," I announce, making sure to mask any pride. The truth is I've been incorporating astrology into my religion, but Mum doesn't need to know that. "You're a Taurus. That means you're stubborn."

Mum laughs, "Who's stubborn? I believe I remember trying to toilet train you, Penn." She sits down on one of the stools at the window-counter. "What else am I, according to the stars?" Since she is not making fun of me and looks genuinely interested, I sit down, too.

"Well, you don't take risks. You're careful and traditional. And," I take a deep inhalation before the next one, "you're secretly very passionate."

The look on Mum's face tells me: I've already ventured too far. For a daughter, I mean. Mum doesn't know about the sorceress part of me, or she might be inclined to listen further. But I think it's best to stop here. She looks terribly... something... Alarmed. And, as if things weren't already tense enough, her admirer marches into the shop, the woman of dubious mental health.

"Can I take a break?" I ask. Mum is already behind the counter, dropping the fish basket into the fryer.

"Sure," she mutters, her back to me. Her ears are red, which means she's probably very angry with me.

As I'm inching out of the shop I hear her admirer saying, "There's something I'd like to ask you..." and I'm even more glad to be making a getaway.

In the Spice House

If I was a smart woman I'd have realized that putting poems into her orders of fish 'n chips was a terrible idea. Didn't she march in here and demand to know why Penny forgot to give her a poem! She's assumed we do it for everyone! There's nothing telepathic about our relationship, I see it now. I thought she was wise to me, that we had a quiet communication going on, but it's been made obvious that I'm wrong. If anything it's a huge embarassment to me. Poems in every order! It's a very good thing *he* never works a shift in here or the damage would have been much greater.

And she wasn't supposed to come in that day. She never comes in on a Wednesday! I'm angry to have missed her for a funeral. And what did Penny think when she was told that we put *poems* in with the fish? Why in heaven did I crawl out onto this limb, start this whole terrible mess? My heart stopped twice: once when she walked in and again when she expressed concern about the poetic inconsistency of her lunch!

One good thing came of it. She introduced herself, gave her *name*. Her complaint was amicable, if confused, and she began it by putting out her hand and saying, "My name's Miranda." Like a bloody schoolgirl I went deaf when she squeezed my hand. Knocked over a bottle of tartar sauce and stuttered my reply to her unheard speech. I gathered enough, I suppose: where was her poem? Was the young girl working here new to the staff? Could I give her *two* poems this time to make up for last time? You can imagine my humiliation as I explained that *we* were all out of poems.

"All out?" she asked, surprised.

I nodded.

"But they're hand-copied. Couldn't you take a moment and write one up for me?" Her concern was great, and she wrinkled her brow, saying, "It's just that I've been putting them up in my office, to cheer myself. The walls in my office are tobacco-brown and I've been covering it up with your pages of poetry. I've only got room for three more and the patches of brown make it look so unfinished!"

What to do! The vision of her surrounded by sheets of my handwriting gave me a half-thrill. I never dreamt that she might keep them. The fact that for a brief time she would hold them in her hands was all I ever hoped for. Even if she doesn't *understand* the message I've been trying to send her, she's been *keeping* them.

"Look, can't *you* write me one?" she asked. She was almost begging, pleading for poetry.

I don't know why, but I shut down then. Told her to put up some photographs or something if the brown patches were bothering her so much. It was almost a lecture, from my point of view, though I was careful not to be too rude or gruff. I just couldn't bear the embarrassment a minute longer. And, to my mind, it is a little out-of-line to expect poems on command! If I was a real Poet myself I'd have been deeply offended. As she was leaving the shop I promised her two for the next time, but it didn't seem to soothe her at all. She looked quite upset.

So, it's off to the library to find more lady poets I guess. Or maybe I *could* scribble up something myself and give it to her under a false name. At least she'd have the impression I was awfully well-read, knowing even the most obscure poets.

PENNY

Duh must be the ugliest man I've ever seen, especially when he's asleep. His mouth hangs open in such a way that any bystander can have intimate knowledge of his dental history. It's the tale of a lost battle with hygiene, of ancient and haphazard drilling and filling. He snores like a chain-saw and smacks his lips every so often. Perhaps he dreams of eating something besides fish and mushy peas. Nothing else ever finds its way into his stomach; no fruit or recognizable vegetable. My Duh may be the finest undocumented case of human scurvy available to science. I should report him and have him dragged off to a lab. In his absence we could actually sit on our own sofa, watch our own TV; if we chose to. The sofa would have to be cleaned first. The upholstery has taken on a texture very similar to margarine from all his sweating and spilling.

One might be inclined to feel sorry for him, but I am beyond anything as affectionate as pity. He may very well be pathetic, but he's also violent, and that is unforgiveable. He's gone out of his way to ruin Mum's life. Once a person has been smacked around they lose hope. If only she'd cuff him right back, just once! But I'm afraid it's too late for retaliation that simple. She feels *sorry* for him. There's no other explanation.

Right after Mum's admirer came into the shop I came here, to the door of the living room. No matter how long I stare at Duh I can't figure it out. An optimist would look at him and say, "There's hope for him yet." A nostalgic would say, "Hidden under all that sweat and spittle there was once a very fine young man." But I feel about my Duh as a demolitionist must feel about a large and obtrusive boulder: he's *in the way* and should most definitely be blown up and out of here. With quiet dynamite.

NAN

I once stood over him with a rolling pin. It seemed like a possibility. But Penn was only a toddler and it seemed self-ish to go to jail and leave her. I used to fantasize about being one of those women, the ones who just go blind with rage and do drastic things. The problem is my rage never quite boils up that far. My trouble is that I'm too level-headed, even in a temper. If only I weren't English. But I suppose there are calm people in every country, people cursed with a freakish and inexplicable tranquility. I'm one such, but to be English makes it worse I think. Or I could blame my mum, who taught me to be polite under every circumstance. Being *classy* she called it. I've never told my Penny to be classy, but I'm afraid she's learning terrible lessons just from watching me.

In a few short years I'll be free to flee. The fantasia of violence that once kept me going has been replaced by other more practical dreams. Now it's the vision of one-day sun and sand that keeps me plugging along. I can't pretend to be completely passive, though. Every time that buzzer rings I feel a brief flash of ambition to murder. But it fades, or gets swallowed, and by the time I'm standing over him with a bottle of beer or his plate of supper, I've forced myself to think of sunsets.

Picture me, though, in the best of both worlds: standing over him in a sarong with a plane ticket in my apron pocket, a rolling pin clenched in my triumphant hands. That would be the ideal scenario of my departure, a quick blow to his skull and a taxi to the airport. But I think I'll probably just pretend to go to the beershop and never come back. Now there's a far-off dream.

PENNY

How great a sin could patricide be? I mean, really, in the scheme of things: why is it deserving of such an ominous title? The word murder becomes rather tame next to *patricide, matricide, infanticide.* Why, even *pesticide* sounds much more tragic than *bugspray*. The best approach would be to expel the word patricide from my mental vocabulary... or would it? The biggest bonus offered by thinking in Latin is the immediately clinical approach. The use of the word patricide allows the removal of one's father from the face of the earth to seem less bloody, less theatrical. It becomes an almost medical duty, doesn't it?

There is also the question of how quickly one should perform the basic procedure. Should it be sudden, an instant thing, or long and painful, to mirror my Duh's languid and sofa-bound sadism? Questions abound when I finally sit down to think about the whole operation. One has to allow questions, yet not permit them to destroy the possibility of action.

Mighty gods, why have you urged me to question? If you kill it, strike me dumb so that I do not continue to lay awake night after night, plagued by inquiries of my own making! I've had to take an entire bottle of headache tablets over the course of this week, not to mention the fact that I've developed a taste for valerian root!

NAN

Someone has been into my special closet, the one where I hide my library books and maps. I thought I'd imagined their disarray, but it's become clear: someone knows of their location. I can't recall which order they were originally stacked in, but today when I went into the cupboard to retrieve the one on Fijian temples, the pile was knocked over. What is strangest about the disturbance is that the cupboard is quite inaccessible, being hidden behind two large rubbish bins. It's in the narrow hall leading to the back alley behind the shop, a corridor used for tossing refuse and little else. Penny sometimes enters the flat through the back door, but she usually prefers to use the shop door.

If it's *him* that's got into my cupboard he hasn't said anything. But he has been known to lay in wait, biding his time when he's suspicious. The last time we had a similar incident was when he came across a sketch-book of mine. I went through a phase of drawing when Penny was in kindergarten: I liked to draw nudes. I'd learned to draw flowers and things in school, but I was fascinated with the idea of nude bodies, especially women's. I hadn't seen any nude women other than myself, not even my mum, and I was curious. So I began drawing pictures of imaginary ladies in the nude and made a terrific effort to have them look very different from myself. Well, he found the book and wasn't pleased. But did he come right out and say so? No. He sat down with a big black crayon and drew clothes over the naked ladies, and that's how I found my book: littered with his untalented scribbles. It was the first and last time I ever lost my temper with him. I was in a real fury after I found it. In those days he was still well enough to go out to the pub on an evening. When he came back in from a night with his mates I pounced on him, sketch-book in hand.

And what did he say? What did he do?

He looked at the book and said, "I don't want that in my house."

"It's art," I said, and I was shaking with rage. Well, it had been art 'til he got hold of it. I kept shaking the sketch-book at him, open to one of his massacres of my drawing. That's when he grabbed it out of my hands and struck me with it. Hit me across the face dozens of times with my own book of drawings! He was never happy 'til he had me crying and apologizing. God knows he never felt the need to apologize for his behaviour. They say some of his kind always apologize, but not *him*. The only person he's ever felt sorry for is himself.

If he's ever given me anything but grief, the words he said that particular night on his way out the door were a kind of gift. In those days he was in the habit of going back out to the pub if we had an *incident*. He stood at the door and glared at me, shaking the crumpled sketch-pad in his hands, its tattered pages flapping and smeared, and he said, "I'll not have *lesbian* drawings in this house!" And though I was terribly upset I felt a kind of joyous *"Ohhhh"* in my heart, a ping of self-recognition. He gave me the word. I've never thanked him properly for the inspiration, the title.

Well, if it is him who has found my secret stash of books, what does he think *this* time? That I'm a closeted archaeologist? A secret-agent of travel? He's seldom wrong, after all.

PENNY

There's been a miracle! At least, I pray there has been some kind of epiphany in this house. I found a bunch of Mum's library books in the hall cupboard, books on Fiji. Could it be that she's planning to run away? That would be a lot to hope for! Of course, it's impossible for me to come right out and ask her. It might prevent her from carrying it out. There were all sorts of them, and maps, too. Why would she be studying maps if she wasn't planning to actually *go?* But then, Bora Bora and Fiji! How on earth will I manage to get her over there?

Normally I'm quite good at snooping, but I heard Duh moving about in the living room and got scared that he would come out and catch me in the cupboard, so I simply shut the door. I'm afraid I left the books in a bit of a mess. There's no time for me to go back and straighten them up unless I get sent back out to put the trash out. It's a job Mum usually performs, and now I know why. I always wondered why she was out there for so long, fiddling around when she's usually quick about most chores. She's been out there reading up on foreign lands!

What a week this has been! First the discovery of Mum's cache of books, then the recurring visits of her admirer, every single day this week and sometimes for both lunch and supper. On two occasions she ate her meal *in the shop.* Mum was there, working alongside me. I tried to make chit-chat with the woman but Mum kept sending me to fetch things from the freezer, so it hasn't been easy to find out if the woman is crazy or not. She's definitely odd: both times she ate here she folded up her newsprint wrapping and put it in her coat pocket instead of putting it in the bin near the door. When I asked Mum if she thought the woman was a bit strange, all Mum said was, "I don't think so. She's always quite nice."

I *did* manage to find out that she's a travel agent. But Mum wasn't in the shop that night, she was off buying beer for Duh. I simply asked her flat out what she does for a living that keeps her at work such long hours. A travel agent! It's too much to bear. I have to figure out a way to tell Mum without seeming too obvious.

Mighty gods! A travel agent! Please let my Mum recognize opportunity staring her right in the face!

NAN

She sells plane tickets for a living, does Miranda. And package bus tours of the flower-beds in the United States. Books all kinds of dream vacations for all kinds of people, but specializes in women's travel, or so she says. *Prefers* to deal with women, she says, and winks at me! What can I say back to her but, "Oh, well, women are quite nice." Imagine! What a thing to say, not at all clever and certainly far from subtle. After this exchange we fall silent and she waits for her fish to come out of the fryer.

Then she says, soft as you please, "I loved the Anne Sexton, but I especially liked the Irma... what's her name again?"

Of course I can't recall a name I made up two nights ago in a panic. Irma... But if I can't remember the names of the poets I choose, she'll think I'm careless, or stupid. It started with a K or something. Was it a French name?

"Kolslavik," she shouts, suddenly remembering for me. "The one about Bora Bora. I loved that one. Have you ever been?"

"Me? No, no," I say, wrapping the fish, embarrassed to have been lured into a chat with her while I'm sneaking another of my own poems into the paper. This time I've used the name Carrie Greer.

Miranda shakes her head, "She captures it perfectly, the sense of isolated paradise. I mean, I've only been to parts of Fiji, but the sky down there is as blue-black as she says it is. That part of the world fascinates me. I'm saving Bora Bora for a real vacation."

"What do you mean, a real one?" I have to say I'm relieved that she hasn't caught on to the fact that I wrote the poem, but I feel a bit badly, tricking her.

She sighs, "I want to go when it's not about work." She takes her packet of fish and holds it up like a trophy, "Who have I got in here today? No—don't tell me. I'll wait 'til I get back to the office. Have a nice night. And *thank-you*."

Oh, Lord. Wait 'til she gets an eyeful of Miss Carrie Greer! I've gone the limit today where shamelessness is concerned. It's an experimental poem, and not very discreet.

It reads something along these lines:

In the Spice House

S.O.S
Whale beached
on the sands
of terror/love/desire
rescue
A.S.A.P.

I regret putting such a ludicrous poem into her lunch. Have I been to Bora Bora? No, darling, I haven't, but I'm just about to visit the end of my rope!

PENNY

The field of actuarial science appeals to me. I've been thinking about careers that would allow me to make full use of my morbidity. Of course my counsellor at school was disgusted by my list of three Dream Jobs: Cosmetologist For The Dead, Actuarial Scientist, and Coroner. She threatened to call my Mum about it. Thought I was being mischievous. I assured her that I was simply following the dictates of astrology and distracted her with a detailed explanation of the Scorpio nature. I then agreed to change my first career choice to Astrologer in an effort to assuage her concerns about my sincerity. I also realized that if I'm to remove Duh from the planet, it wouldn't do to leave a paper trail such as a Dream Jobs list littered with death-related professions. In fact, I think I'll change everything on the list. Also, an appointment with my so-called Guidance Counsellor will allow me to miss gym, a class which sickens me to the marrow.

The idea of studying actuarial science came upon me when I was examining Duh's life insurance policies. He keeps some of his private papers hidden in the sofa. Luckily my Mum is listed as his sole beneficiary. There's no one else, I suppose, since Duh has never gotten along with his family very well. Apparently they're a deeply religious group of fanatics, which may be where I've gotten my own tendency toward piety, though I'm not fanatical, just faithful. Anyway, from what I could decipher from Duh's policies, Mum could profit from his demise in a financial sense, not to mention a spiritual one. I didn't have enough time to take the kind of detailed notes I like to, but I got the basics down in my head. She gets it all, and that's what matters. It would be good if I could get a look at his will, too. I didn't see it with his other papers, but I was in a bit of a rush. There's no casual way to ask Mum if the wills are kept someplace handy without raising her suspicions. I'll simply have to wait until he's in the loo and have another look under the sofa cushions.

I think a career based on calculating how long a person is likely to live would be fascinating. But then people like my Duh would present a bit of a challenge.

Mighty gods, please ensure that when my Duh settles back down onto his precious sofa that he is not like the Princess and the Pea, noticing the slightest disarray beneath the cushions. And please let his Will and Testament be hidden in the sofa!

NAN

I can't help wondering why it is that I'm convinced things will ever change. That I will suddenly one day be able to take charge of my life after living this way for years. Is it blind hope? Dangerous fantasy?

I find myself speculating about what *she* does with her days and nights, and why *her* life is so different from mine. Before she ever came into the shop I'd begun my plans for escape, but there's a new urgency, now that *she* is around. It never used to occur to me to compare my days and nights with those of anyone else. And if she knew anything about me she'd probably feel nothing but disgust, discovering as she would that I've let life happen to me instead of me happening to it. How do I have the nerve to imagine that anything will change when my greatest act of courage was getting a library card and memorizing information about places I fancy I'll visit?

No, *she* wouldn't live this life. I can tell by the way she walks and talks. She'd never watch her life tick on, measured by the thousands of wire baskets plunged in and pulled out of oil. This is the first time I have felt complete despair. Nothing is going to *happen*. Me gazing at atlases and feeling grand attachments to foreign countries isn't going to make *him* go away. Lately I've dreamt of just leaning over the counter and telling her, "I'm dying, I have a terrible disease, please help me." And I picture her valiant response, how she would take my hand and pull me out of Frye's and lead me to the airport. Telling such lies isn't kind; it's cowardly. But is it so far from the truth? Because, you see, it struck me today, leaning over the fryer, that even a piece of soggy halibut has more energy than me. And I realized: I *am* dying, or have been dead for years. It's just that no one's pronounced me.

In brief flickering moments *she* seems to resuscitate me. But I'm beginning to hate those moments; I'm teased into thinking my wildest dreams are possible.

PENNY

This one is pure extract. He'll not have the strength to reach for his beloved buzzer. Time enough, perhaps, to feel unusual, to feel suspicious. Saturday afternoon, his head full of football, his gizzard plugged with beer. And then he'll have pain like he's never known, but no one will help him. The shop will be busy, the volume of the TV drowning out his pathetic cries for help. I've got it all ready, and Mum expects me in the shop now. I'll keep myself close to the magic bowl, twin of the other. It won't be easy to manage it. But I've worked it out. One of my sub-gods supplied me with the choreographics of it last night.

Mighty gods, please allow me the courage to carry out my plan without the interference of conscience. Let my shadow-self preside over the entire affair. Let nothing obscure this execution if it is meant to be. You have chosen me, by virtue of my very birth, to be the one who frees my Mum. Amen.

NAN

Penny seems unwell to me today. Perhaps she slept badly. She's a secret worrier I think. I'd hoped to ask her if she thinks I'm dead, but the shop is busy and her mood tells me I shouldn't be selfish, asking such worrisome questions. She insists on working the fryer, tells me she's tired of being the one to run the cash register. We've always done it that way, on Saturdays; I cook and she rings in the purchases. But she's bored, and I can understand that. If I had my way she wouldn't work here at all, but I need the help. God knows *he'd* never allow me to hire someone from outside the family. It might cost him real money.

I've a letter in my pocket, though. Penny's insistence that she run the fryer makes it difficult for me to pass along. I'll have to slip it into the bag instead of wrapping it in the newsprint. If she comes in, that is. I've been thrown off by her inconsistent visits of late. Never comes on the same few days anymore, always on a different day, sometimes twice in one day, lunch and supper. The one thing I can count on is Penn having her back to me while she cooks. But if *Miranda* doesn't even come in then I've nothing to worry about. I hope that she does not come in, or that she'll come later, after I've dismissed Penny for the day.

"When's Duh having his lunch?" asks Penny.

"I don't know, he hasn't said. Why?"

Penny screws her face up and shrugs, "I'll take it to him is all. Save you the trouble. I know how he is when he's watching football. I don't mind." Am I imagining that Penny looks almost green today? She's not the most robust girl at the best of times, especially since she gave up eating meat, but today she is definitely pale and quite grumpy.

"Are you all right, Penn?" I ask, but then the door of the shop bangs and it is *her*. Penny grunts something and damned if the buzzer doesn't go off at the same moment. I'm torn. "Would you go see what your Duh wants, Penn?"

"He wants his lunch," she says, quite flatly. I didn't hear the number of buzzes, but I'm sure he's not asking for his lunch this early. I tell Penny to go and see, thinking it's my perfect chance. I don't wish it upon her to be engaged in a conversation with him, but it would allow me to take over the fryer while *she's* here.

"Hello," Penny says, addressing Miranda with sudden brightness. "How are things at the agency today?" I'm surprised by Penny's familiarity with the woman.

"Oh, fine," says Miranda. I stand foolishly silent and helpless, the letter in my pocket.

"This lady's a travel agent, Mum," Penny smiles, and when the buzzer goes off again she sticks her tongue out at the speaker and says, plain as you please, and as though Miranda is an old friend, "We've got an invalid on the premises."

She turns her back, leaving me to gaze in embarrassment at the expectant face of Miranda the Travel Agent. Penny is ignoring the buzzer, busy dipping fish, presumably for her Duh.

"Someone sick you have to look after?" Miranda asks, in the same soft voice she says *thank-you* with.

There's a terrible crash behind me and Penny shouts, "Clumsy twit!" There's batter all over the floor and she begins to wipe at it furiously, cursing herself, saying, "Sorry, Mum." My theory that she is out of sorts today must be correct: her face is flushed and she is knocking things about.

"Will you have your usual lunch today?" I ask Miranda, glancing back at Penny who is now staring intently into the fryer. When the buzzer sounds again she reaches over and unplugs it. "Penny, after you've finished making your Duh's lunch, take a nice long break, hey? You don't seem well today." Penny shrugs and Miranda waits patiently for the confusion to subside.

"Just coleslaw today," she says. That's grand. How on earth will I sneak the letter in now, bury it in the mayonnaise? It isn't meant to be. I must look crestfallen, because Miranda suddenly announces that she'll have fish.

"Good, because I've already put your order in," says Penny smugly, turning to smile at me.

And then *he* bellows from the hallway, startling both Penny and I. It won't do to have him come in here, not with *her* standing in the shop! In a panic I give Penny a shove on the arm and hiss, "Will you go see what your Duh wants? Please?" Penny stands chewing her lip and knits her eyebrows, but his bellowing is approaching the shop door. It won't do! Miranda has moved to the window-counter, perhaps sensing the possibility of a family row.

Flinging the back door wide, Penny shouts, "Lunch is coming Duh! Hold on!" and slams it shut again. She knows he won't tolerate shouting, not when it's anyone else! I can't understand her behaviour at all today. It's bizarre, the way she's peering into the fryer and looking all flustered. The door opens a crack and he pushes his ugly head through.

"I want a beer as well," he says, to no one in particular. And I am ashamed to have him ordering us about in front of Miranda.

"Are you really that crippled?" I bark, without thought for the consequences. I can count the occasions when I've spoken up to him on one hand, but my shame moves me to fury.

"Wha?" he spits, taken aback. His eyes narrow and I'm afraid he'll come right into the shop. I move to the fryer and begin to reach for the basket, hoping Miranda's fish is ready. But Penny won't let me get at the handle.

"It's all right, Duh, I'll bring you a beer. Mum's busy is all," Penny says, sweetly and without any trace of anger, though she's quite hostile about me coming near the fryer.

"At least someone looks after me," he nods, and slams the door with finality.

"Let me get Miranda's fish up, hon," I say, trying to be pleasant. But I feel terribly hurt by Penny's undermining way with her Duh. She's the only person I can count on for absolute loyalty, and here she is placating him, kissing his bottom.

"Mum!" she snaps. "Let me do my bloody job!" But she stands puzzling over the fish-basket, looking from one piece to the other, acting confused by her simple task. I hope she isn't pregnant! She's behaving as though she could be.

I snatch the handle of the basket and turn the fish over onto the cloth we keep spread out to soak up excess grease. I'll play along with Penn. "Which one is your Duh's?" I ask.

"The big piece," she whispers, and takes it up, eyeing it critically. Miranda is still seated at the window-counter and can't hear us, though I'm sure the fact that we are whispering makes her wonder.

"Here," says Penny, handing me the second piece of fish with her *fingers*. She takes a plate down from a shelf and plops her Duh's fish onto it, adding chips from the heated pan. I begin to wrap up Miranda's halibut, embarrassed by its smallness, and when Penny trudges away with her Duh's lunch in hand, I reach for the letter.

It's a bulky thing, a frightening pack of pages to give someone I hardly know. But I *must* give it. Swooping down into quiet despair is not useful. Only action is useful. It occurred to me in sleep last night, and I got up and wrote three long pages in the loo. *Dear Miranda*. Heart on the sleeve of the hand I wrote with. There's terror in me as I bury it in the newsprint wrapping, but gladness, too. Maybe she just won't come back again after reading it; there's a kind of accomplishment in that. And then I'll know she's been reading poems for the sake of poetry and not out of unsaid love.

She notices me wrapping the fish and smiles, "There's my fortune cookie for today. It's wonderful that you do that."

"Is it?" I ask, annoyed with my timid whisper of a voice.

"Oh, yeah. No one else would think to do it. It's clever. Makes the food taste even better. *Thank-you*."

Penny slips back into the shop despite my instructions for her to rest. She stands behind me fiddling with the sheets of newsprint. Of course she has no idea why I'd like to be in the shop alone. Miranda nods and takes her meal, unaware of what she carries in her hand. And when she goes out the door I am suddenly filled with terrible regret.

"How was Duh?" I ask Penn, hoping to bring things back to a normal state. I shouldn't be so quick to judge the poor child's loyalty. She copes the best she can.

Penny snorts, "Says he's tired. The walk from the living room probably did him in." She raises her eyes to mine and adds, very quietly, "I love you, Mum."

There's no time to be touched by Penn's out-of-character announcement. Some workmen come in and we remain busy for the entire afternoon and evening. The buzzer does not go off and Penny seems far less rattled. Until I announce that I'm going to go back to the flat to check on *him*.

"Leave the bastard," she says firmly, and I remember that she has unplugged the intercom. Perhaps she has reached her limit with her Duh.

PENNY

Horror has struck. A horror worse than anything imaginable. After a patient afternoon and evening in the shop with Mum, we went back to the kitchen for tea. And who was sitting on the sofa, wide awake and glowering at us both as we passed by the door? Duh! It's just not possible. The poison was pure extract, and lots of it! What might have happened is unbearable to contemplate. If I made some kind of terrible error I will have ruined my Mum's life! I never expected the confusion, I thought I knew exactly which piece it was!

Mighty gods, please make the poison work if it was Duh's piece. Please make it powerless if it was not his piece but hers... Perhaps I am not the chosen one after all...

NAN

I'm useless, he says, and cruel. Forcing a poor man to humiliate himself in his own shop. He should have known, he says, that at heart I'm nothing but a witch. I've taught Penny to hate him, he says. Child abuse, he decides, that's what I've committed by poisoning her mind. A girl needs her father, he says, but I've made sure she doesn't like him. The tongue lashing goes on and on. But he does not raise his hand to me, instead, he weeps. Blubbers and spits and complains, but he doesn't move to violence. He expects an apology for all I've done today, and for all I didn't do. Don't I know it's hard for him to come near the shop door and hear me running his business into the ground ? He knows what is going on, he says. If it weren't for his illness he could put a stop to it. And as he goes on and on about my malicious destruction of his business, his empire of halibut, I feel myself go deliciously numb. I can't forget that what inspired this tirade was a refusal to answer his buzzings this afternoon. And it's delightful in a way, to be able to remember that his unanswered request for a beer is all that it takes to trigger a litany.

Having somewhere listened all these years, and half-believed his criticisms, and soaked up his hatred, his blame: I feel tremendously proud of myself just now. A bottle of beer is what it's about. My incompetence is not the cause. While such an epiphany may seem late in coming, and rather basic, it makes me feel glad. Glad to have written that letter and glad that Penny ignored my urgings to answer him. Something in the sour air of the living room is crackling with change.

"Sorry, Jim," I say, and head for the stairs.

He shouts, "It isn't so easy! It's not all that simple, woman!"

I continue my ascension of the staircase and whisper, "Oh, but it *is*."

PENNY

Mighty gods, please end this torture. The days and nights pass and Miranda does not appear in the shop. Mum is more and more despondent. I can't have ruined it all! Please, please, the unknown is too much for my faith just now. I've read all the books I can on poison, I was sure of my expertise; and now I may have killed Mum's only catalyst for freedom. Answer this prayer: is Miranda dead? Have I made a terrible error? Why did you allow the forces of distraction to make me fail? Is there a reason? Was Miranda a devil, or lacking power? Was she worse than my Duh, an imposter? It's been days and days since she's come around. Help me, mighty gods, send me a signal to indicate my sin...

NAN

She's read it and fled. There's nothing to do but cry a little and shrug off the humiliation. But it bites, it does, the shame of my confession. For I went the whole distance, claiming love at first sight, confessing to the truth that no one else receives poems in their lunch. I told her to re-read them all, to see the evidence. It's awful to know she's walking around with my heart. That she could be going elsewhere for lunch out of discomfort, or disgust. I told her about *him*, the miserable truth, my dreams of Bora Bora. Spilled myself out in carefully written words. I left nothing to the imagination except my fantasies. I didn't want her to think of me as a pornographer, after all.

He doesn't let up, either. He's broken all my knick-knacks and has begun working on the living room lamps. All's quiet and then there is a crash. I've told Penny to steer clear of him and let me answer his frequent buzzings. Oh, he's buzzing with a fury now, expecting full-service every ten minutes. He called me in to turn a page of the TV guide yesterday. No one would believe me, but his incessant beckoning is worse than any beating. He's taken to waking me up from a sound sleep to demand answers to his questions. Why am I so stupid, he asks, why am I so ugly? I tricked him with my beauty, he insists.

Penny is behaving even more oddly, her mood a mixture of irritability and melancholy. She's asked to work every day, saying she needs a break from school. I can't seem to screw up the courage to ask her if she's pregnant. She refuses to leave the shop until we've closed up at night.

One evening, out of the blue, she said, "I'm sorry Mum." When I asked her what she was sorry for she burst out crying and shook her head. No amount of pleading would have her tell me what was wrong.

And then today, just as suddenly, she announced that she needed the day off. It's Saturday of course, our busiest day, but I can't bear to ask her to work. Whatever is troubling her is making her more and more pale. Instead of reading books on foreign lands I should be reading up on adolescents. It's clear I'm going about mothering in all the wrong ways. When she was little I could ask her things, but now, well, she's off in a world of her own most of the time. She's far away as Bora Bora, and it's her I should be trying to reach, not some imagined paradise.

PENNY

Maybe Miranda will come into the shop while I'm away from it. There could be some aspect of my energy that is driving her away. I can't cope with the idea that I may have poisoned her. I've planned a full day of wandering around town and have decided to purchase another vial of poison. He has to be removed. If I have to pour it down his throat myself I will.

NAN

I've gone and committed a terrible sin, the worst any mother could. When Penny was out I went into her room to have a look through her things. Because I read that secrecy in a teenager could be drug-related. And it seems to be worse than I imagined. There *are* strange powders in her drawers, and books on the devil. Confronting her will be difficult, because I'll have to admit to snooping around. I left things as I found them, even the strange little bottles of powdery substance. But I can't ignore the truth. She needs help.

The strangeness of this household is wearing me down. Didn't he suddenly announce his intention to spend the evening at the pub! He showered and shaved and behaved in other alarming ways. Took a handful of money from the register and blew me a kiss on his way out the front door of the shop. There's a football pool, I thought to myself. And it just figures according to my poor luck that the night he treats me to his absence is the night when Penny has disappeared. She hasn't called, and I'm stuck here in the shop. I suppose I could just close down for the evening in honour of his energetic departure, but fear prevents me. Things are bad enough without adding to them. It is in this slavish way that I preserve myself by avoiding trouble when I can.

PENNY

The shop's black, closed up. Mum usually keeps it open 'til midnight on Saturdays, but maybe she was tired. But wait, the flat is dark, too. I stumble up the steps to my room where my lamp is on. I did not leave it on. There's a note on my pillow. Mum's handwriting.

Stay here in the flat, lovey. Something has happened, and I need you to be home when I get back. It may be late. Go to sleep and I'll wake you. Love, Mum.

The handwriting is not Mum's usual gorgeous script. It's quivery. From the reading I've done on graphology I can see that she is upset. There is evidence of an attempt to control her hand. Well, I will not sleep. Duh's not here, Mum's not here... It's something terrible, I can feel it. He's never not here, and Mum was supposed to be running the shop.

I will *not* sleep. Because when Duh gets home I'm going to make sure he has a cup of tea with lots of milk and sugar, and a little something else. He's done something terrible to her. And yet I know that he'll come marching back into this house, somehow forgiven by Mum. Maybe she finally called the police on him.

NAN

How to tell her. I never expected to feel this way. So shocked and unprepared. I was going to pack a suitcase one day and leave him to go on... They told me he won the football pool, and was happy. Was dancing and drinking like he hasn't for years. The joy was too much for his miserable heart and he fell in the toilet. Instantly dead, they said, because of the excitement. A young fellow found him sprawled on the floor of a stall. Strange to be comforted by strangers, consoled by a bartender. They were all at the hospital, milling around red-faced. I don't feel anything. But shock is acceptable.

He won five hundred dollars and that was enough to cripple his greedy heart.

I've got the envelope of money in my lap, riding home to Penny. How to tell her.

PENNY

Mum taps softly on my door. I don't bother to hide my books nor the vials of spider-belly extract. When she comes in she eyes the incense burning on my dresser but says nothing, sits on the bed beside my copy of the Satanic bible, oblivious.

"What is it Mum?" I ask, relieved that she isn't covered with injuries, at least not ones I can see. "Where's Duh?" I expect her to mutter that he's in the living room, but she doesn't.

"Your Duh has passed away, Penn," she says, and I can't believe the movement of her mouth through these words.

"What?" I shout, and disbelief prevents the emergence of my glee.

"He was happy, they said. Went down to the pub and won a football pool. He had a heart attack. It was mostly painless," she sighs.

That's too bad, I think. It's not possible for me to hide my blossoming grin, and Mum sees it and looks shocked. I can't help it, my prayers have been answered, though not in complete accordance with my requests.

"Are you high?" Mum asks, putting a hand on my arm, searching my face with her eyes. She hasn't been crying, her eyes are clear and green.

"High?" I laugh. Mum thinks I'm *on* something, so under the influence of stimulants that I could be happy about Duh's death. "No, I'm not high. Why d'you think I'm high?"

Mum motions toward the little vials of powders.

Now's not the time to tell her that I've been practicing the art of poisoning in hopes of killing Duh. She may still be in denial, or sad via some moral mode of grief. I tell her that the powders are bath-salts and protest against her assumption that I could even *try* drugs, although I *have*.

Telling her about the tattoo is a simpler matter. She points to it and raises her brows. Though it's a queer design and one that screams religion, Mum examines my hand with admiration, tells me it's lovely. She supposes all the kids at school have them now. Well, not quite this sort...

We sit up all night drinking Relaxation Tea. The house is so quiet without the TV roaring. At five or six a.m. Mum announces that she needs to go to bed. There'll be a lot to do, she says. When I hear her door close I creep into the living room and unplug the buzzer that he kept next to the sofa. I let myself into the shop and turn the fryer on, content to watch the oil as it heats up. When it's good and hot I take the buzzer from his Throne and the buzzer from the shop and throw them both into the smoking oil.

Mighty gods, he was a misery. Thank-you for your generosity.

NAN

It seems a blur, a dreamlike week. Sitting in offices, signing papers and making arrangements; it *is* me doing it all, looking after things, but I can't quite believe his absence. Though I have looked after things for ages, I always had the shadow of his disapproval hovering over me, waiting for me on the sofa, defining me.

He's not waiting there now. The smell of him still hangs in the living room, but there's no lump of body and shout of voice. Nothing of him but the fading stench of sweat and a few empty bottles in the pantry, waiting for return but not for replenishment. Penny is the one exhibiting obvious relief. She's cheerful and keen to help, showing no signs of grief. She has every reason to feel relieved, of course, but her jolly temperament makes me wonder if it hasn't quite sunk in yet.

In the Spice House

I sat through the funeral feeling quite unusual, fighting nervous laughter. It was, in many ways, no more upsetting than attending old Forester's funeral. But tears *have* come to me. Only they aren't the tears of widowhood. They're tears of unbearable regret. Watching Penny move gaily about the flat has shown me I was wrong to think divorce would have been too much for her. Perhaps it was too much for *me*.

I'm grateful to have the daughter that I do. She has saved me from the idea that I should keep Frye's going. In her mind selling the business is the only option. Without her saying so, I think she knows how very trapped I am. It never occurred to me that his death would mean the end of Frye's Fish and Chippery. I've been the one to run it for so long that I suppose I thought it was mine to continue. Until it's sold I plan to keep it open for business. Penn insists that we have to repaint the sign out front so that it reads: MADAME Frye's Fish and Chippery. She'll look after it, she says, unless I'd find it therapeutic to do it myself. But I tell her to go ahead, that I've plenty to keep me busy. Ordering newsprint and things. One can't be wallowing in therapeutics when there's money to be made. He didn't leave behind a fortune, and income is necessary. For college and trips and things. Penn might fancy another tattoo, or a visit to the dermatologist. I don't want to deny her anything anymore.

We've cleaned the entire flat, upstairs and down. It was a cathartic task, throwing his belongings out. Again it was Penn who suggested it. I needed to locate a few of his papers for dealings with the lawyer. We split the duties, Penn taking the upstairs bedroom and me going over the living room. That's how I found his Will, shoved under the sofa-cushions. It was badly stained; he'd hidden a piece of fish under the cushions and the grease soaked through the pages. His piggishness knew no bounds. Imagine,

188

shoving a piece of perfectly good fish under the cushions where he sat! It was a rotten smelling thing by the time I found it. I wonder, did he have no sense of smell left? But then, he wasn't the most pleasantly aromatic creature himself.

Anyway, with the burial achieved (and it is an achievement, I can admit that to myself) we've only to sell the business. And then what? All the library books in the world don't seem to hold the answer. In the whirl of duties generated by his sudden demise, I forgot about Miranda. It wasn't 'til I was sitting in the funeral home that she popped into my head. Rather timely, I guess, because I fell into a fit of weeping that must have seemed like absolute bereavement. It was.

PENNY

I should feel bad but I don't, not about Duh. He's in the ground with the other worms. My biggest sorrow is the death of Miranda. She has not come into the shop. I came right out and asked Mum about all kinds of things the night after the funeral. And she did the same with me. It seems there were lots of questions between us. She wanted to know the strangest things: was I *active*, was I pregnant, a drug abuser? It was my behaviour that made her wonder, she said. Apparently I was pale and jittery and more distant than usual. When I told her about my private religion she wasn't alarmed at all. She just said, "Everyone needs something to believe in."

That's when I said, "Like Bora Bora?"

Her face! She blushed blood-red and said, "It was you looking through my books!"

And then she told me how she's been dreaming of running away for years. It didn't bother me. She's taught herself Spanish and French, in hopes of travelling one day. All from books. And all in secret. I had no idea Mum was so full of secrets. Had no idea that Miranda was one of them. *Was?* Oh, there was no way for me to confess that I poisoned Mum's *objet d'amour*. When she said Miranda doesn't come into the shop anymore, just out of the blue like that, I saw how sad she is about it. She is sadder about Miranda than about Duh. That's not really very surprising to me. I've always known that my Mum fancied women. And Duh didn't deserve any tears, though he inspired plenty when he was alive.

"I can't talk about Miranda just now," said Mum, and she went up to her room, ending our mutual confessional.

We're going to keep the shop going for a bit 'til we can sell it. I don't mind working alongside Mum except that every time I go near the fryer it reminds me that I am a murderer. Even my religion hasn't helped me cope with the idea that I've killed my Mum's chances of Love. I have to shut my ears against the sound of the fish dropping into the oil.

Mighty gods, please send Passion in its fullest force toward my Mum. She deserves to know it at least once.

NAN

Now, more than ever, my entire life is this bloody chip-shop. I've started slamming things about to blow off steam. I can't hold it in anymore; my hatred of it is far from subtle. Because I no longer care about *his* critiques, or that *he'll* hear of a complaint, I'm far from pleasant. There's no need to worry about whether the salt shakers are clean and my life doesn't depend on the perfection of something as dull as coleslaw. Sod it all, that's what I say. I've cut the hours back as well. My feet can't take the standing anymore, and why should they? No, I like to be seated on the sofa with a cup of tea by half eight in the evenings. We had the sofa shampooed, so that Penn and I could enjoy what's left of its springs.

Today I've decided to shut down at six. Everyone assumes the erratic hours are the result of my being in mourning. I tell Penny to start packing up the rubbish, that we'll take the night off, and she looks pleased. Ever since she and I had a big heart-to-heart (her whole one shared with my shattered scrap of heart) she's been very chatty. She even jokes that she's glad her Duh died before she had to kill him herself. I know that feeling well.

But I'm not prepared for it when *she* walks in, tanned as a surfer, her arms full of flowers, a smile on her lips. Miranda. And would she look that happy if she hated me? Penny makes a choking sound and drops an entire bottle of malt vinegar to the tiles, smashing it completely.

"Hello there," says Miranda, and she holds the bunch of flowers out to *me*. "How've you been?"

"Duh's dead!" blurts Penny, before I can tell of our recent loss. She shouts it from the floor where she is mopping up the broken glass with a rag.

Miranda's smile fades instantly and she stares at me, muttering, "I'm sorry, I had no idea. Oh dear, bad timing on my part..."

Penny pops up like a Jack-in-the-Box, "It's so good to see you back. We were worried." I can't quite fathom why Penn would be worried about Miranda's whereabouts but there's no time to question. I have to *say* something. I just wish Penny would disappear for a minute or two.

"Penn, would you mind taking the rubbish out?" I ask, trying to sound very casual and even a bit matronly about it all. She nods and drags the bags out the back door without a word, humming to herself. I stand helplessly in front of Miranda, staring at my fingers.

"Are you all right?" she asks, *thank-you* soft. "I've been away. I didn't have time to tell you I was going, because I left the night I got your letter."

"Where did you go?" I ask, hoping to change the subject, hoping to control my breathing while she tells of her trip. She's lovely and brown, just like I imagined she would get in the sun. It makes her eyes look wonderfully pale. It sickens me that she looks even more beautiful than before.

"Australia," she says. Is she apologetic? She goes on, "I was investigating some hotels and things."

The flowers are laying on the counter and I thank her for them. There seems to be nothing to say, and I can hear Penny marching toward the shop door, still humming. I cough lightly and say, "Did you want something to eat?"

She reaches into her pocket and pulls out a business card which she lays on the bunch of flowers. "Call me when you're feeling up to it. I was hoping we could have dinner sometime. I have some great books on the Islands."

"The islands?" I ask, trying to sound confused, because Penny is now standing next to me at the counter, sniffing at the flowers and studying Miranda's card.

"You know, Mum, like the ones you want to visit someday," Penny whispers loudly, as though Miranda can't hear from two feet away. Miranda blushes a little and Penny continues, much to my horror. "Would you like to come over for a meal? We've gotten rid of the invalid now. Or how about now? Come in for a drink! Eh, Mum, why don't we close up and have a drink with Miranda?"

How much does Penny know about all this, and how? I stare at her to avoid meeting Miranda's gaze. It's as though they are both waiting for me to answer. And then, as though I no longer exist, Penny says to Miranda, "We never got to have a wake, you see. It'd be good if you could tell Mum how to get a plane ticket and all that."

"I'm sure she knows how to get a plane ticket," smiles Miranda, "but I could help her decide where to go." These two! Conspiring against my shyness.

"Bora Bora's where she wants to go," pipes Penny, tugging at my sleeve as though to wake me.

"Really?" asks Miranda, and I'm grateful for her understanding of the situation. She's sussed out the confusion of the missing poems now, has my letter to fill in any blanks that existed. "Well, let's have a drink then. Should I go to the store?"

"Here's money," says Penny very authoritatively, "my Duh must've known he was going to die, because he drank every drop of liquor in the house. See you in a bit?" It's all settled, in Penny's mind, as Miranda leaves the shop. When the door bangs shut Penny turns to me and says, "I'm afraid I'll have to back out of the party, Mum. I have loads of homework I haven't been looking after."

And she leaves me, sitting in the shop waiting for Miranda to come back with some kind of liquor or other. I haven't had a drink since the shandy at Forester's funeral. I put the flowers in water and turn the lights out in the shop to discourage customers. It seems unreal to me that we'll be sitting on that sofa, Miranda and I, talking about Bora Bora. As though any of it were possible!

I owe a great deal to my Penny, and to Fate. And to Bora Bora, just for being there.

PENNY

Mighty gods, thank-you for your divine work. I can hear my Mum laughing in the living room with her Admirer. In keeping with my Scorpio nature I sit at the top of the stairs for a time and listen. They are talking about poetry and adventure and then I have to strain to hear: Miranda is telling my Mum that she has the most beautiful hands on earth. That she could be a hand-model. And she could!

One last request, oh mighty ones, please give me the good fortune to avoid any future dealings with halibut. It's always left a bad taste in my mouth. And I don't enjoy these spots, vain and unimportant as it may seem. I'm after a little passion myself!

NAN

She calls me Madame, and I think it suits me.

April Fool's Day

Australia's greatest storyteller gives you his most powerful and passionate story yet: the story of Bryce Courtenay's son Damon and his death from medically-acquired AIDS on April 1st, 1991.

April Fool's Day changed Australian law in connection to the handling of blood products as Bryce Courtenay revealed an incompetent system ill-prepared to handle the problems created by the emergence of the HIV virus. His son Damon was a hemophiliac who acquired HIV through a tainted transfusion. Courtenay details how Australian authorities tried to sweep the issue under the rug and turn their backs on the afflicted.

But *April Fool's Day* is much more than an account of incompetence chillingly similar to the situation in Canada today. It is a remarkable love story of the passionate and enduring love between Damon and his partner Celeste who cared for him through to the bitter end. It is also an extraordinary insight into a family coping with hemophilia and AIDS.

April Fool's Day will do many things for you. It is controversial—it will make you angry. It is funny—it will make you laugh. It will certainly make you cry. Above all, it will make you feel the incredible strength love can give—how when we confront our worst, we can become our best.

'Bryce Courtenay has left a lasting memorial to his son, one which thousands have already embraced: chosen as one of the best books of 1995!'—*Vancouver Sun*

Directions for an Opened Body

At times savage, at times sympathetic, this is a collection of images from the charred remains of a series of broken lives. In fourteen stories, Kenneth J. Harvey lays open the intimate preoccupations of ordinary folk captured in extraordinary circumstances. With language by turns banged home like rivets, by turns as delicate as late orange light of day, *Directions for an Opened Body* offers us stories to blaze in memory like firelight, and echo with the breath of the land and sea.

Nominated for the Commonwealth Writers Prize, acclaimed in England, Australia and Canada, *Directions for an Opened Body* is an astonishing first book.

'Harvey is obviously a writer of prodigious talent.'—*The Globe & Mail*

'A formidable presence on the Canadian literary scene... sheer virtuosity.'—*Canadian Book Review Annual*

'An original and arresting talent.'—Alan Ross, *London Magazine*

Born in St. John's in 1962, **KENNETH J. HARVEY** was raised in a Newfoundland very different from the rosy glow of the popular image. Ken Harvey did not meet anyone who fished for a living until his teens and so grew sick of seeing Newfoundlanders depicted as fishermen with quaint houses and colourful speech patterns. Studying at Memorial University in St. John's, Harvey majored in psychology and minored in philosophy. He has won over a dozen awards for Arts & Letters in his native Newfoundland for fiction, poetry, non-fiction, photography and drama.

MINERVA
Stands out from the crowd!

THE ORDER FORM

Qty.	Book Title ISBN	Price	Total
	Bill Bryson		
	Notes from a Small Island . .0433398493	$15.99	
	Neither Here nor There 0749398159	$13.99	
	Bryce Courtenay		
	April Fool's Day 0433398485	$17.99	
	Louis de Bernieres		
	Captain Corelli's Mandolin .0749398574	$13.99	
	War of Emmanuel's		
	Nether Parts 0749391308	$13.99	
	Senor Vivo & the Coca Lord 0749399627	$13.99	
	The Troublesome Offspring		
	of Cardinal Guzman 0749398574	$13.99	
	Roddy Doyle		
	Paddy Clarke Ha Ha Ha 0433391162	$11.99	
	The Barrytown Trilogy 0433391189	$15.99	
	The Commitments 0749391685	$11.99	
	The Snapper 0749336145	$11.99	
	The Van 0749399902	$11.99	
	Kenneth J. Harvey		
	Directions for an		
	Opened Body 0433397543	$15.99	
	James Kelman		
	How late it was, how late . .0433393971	$14.99	
	V.S. Naipaul		
	A Way in the World 0433397110	$15.99	
	Keith Oakley		
	The Case of Emily V. 0433392398	$13.99	
	Irvine Welsh		
	Trainspotting 0749336501	$13.99	
	Marnie Woodrow		
	In the Spice House 0433398386	$16.99	

REED BOOKS CANADA

plus $3.00 shipping & handling	
plus 7% GST	
TOTAL	